>>BOOK THREE OF THE DEERWHERE CODEX<<

EVER AEQUUM
Tales from Deerwhere

J.W. Capek &
James Lowell Snyder

Ever Aequum
Copyright 2020, 2022
by J.W. Capek and James Lowell Snyder

First eBook Edition June 2020
First Print Edition June 2020
Second eBook Edition March 2022
Second Print Edition March 2022

Cover art by David Mecklenburg

ISBN 978-1-59092-952-0

Blue Forge Press is the print division of the volunteer-run, federal 501 (c)3 nonprofit company, Blue Legacy, founded in 1989 and dedicated to bringing light to the shadows and voice to the silence. We strive to empower storytellers across all walks of life with our four divisions: Blue Forge Press, Blue Forge Films, Blue Forge Gaming, and Blue Forge Records. Find out more at www.MyBlueLegacy.org

Blue Forge Press
7419 Ebbert Drive Southeast
Port Orchard, Washington 98367
blueforgepress@gmail.com
360-550-2071 ph.txt

The Decades of Chaos finally whimpered to a close. The 24th Century survived the Pandemic, the wars, the global conflicts, the overpopulation, and natural disasters. The colony of Deerwhere awakened each day to the Recovery of civilization, to the benefits of Peace; meaningful work and labor, service to others, recreation. Together, new civic units were orchestrated by the Quantum computer with female, male, and uniale components. Uniales are the third gender who embody all the maleness and femaleness of the human genome. Through epigenetics, they have the best qualities of both sexes and all the races. Immune to pandemics, Uniales became the crucial element of the civilized earth—the key to dystopian Recovery.

This third novel in *The Deerwhere Codex* was released in summer of 2020. Titled *Ever Aequum*, the codex is a collection of stories related to the Deerwhere experience and recovery from the Chaos of the 21st Century pandemic and wars. Crossing elements of time, the anthology explores the lives, passions, adventures and loves of the uniales, males, females, and quantum computer intelligence. Will three sexes co-exist? Does quantum intelligence recognize sexuality? How do humans survive their natural catastrophes? Uniales become the crucial element of the civilized earth—the key to dystopian Recovery in *Ever Aequum*.

Co-authored by J.W. Capek and James Lowell Snyder with cover art by David Mecklenburg, all books are available in print and eBook format.

ACKNOWLEDGMENTS

Book Three of *The Deerwhere Codex* was written to answer the questions and requests of friends, and family members, and supportive authors.

APPRECIATION IS TOO SMALL A WORD FOR THE SUPPORT THIS NOVEL HAS RECEIVED: Kitsap Literary Artists & Writers, Bremerton Kitsap Access Television, Blue Forge Press, C.B.C. Critique—and a legion of friends who continue to add joy to the writing endeavor.

>>TABLE OF CONTENTS<<

ALSO BY THE AUTHOR

THE DEERWHERE CODEX

Book 1: The Deerwhere Awakening

Book 2: Adrion's Passage

Book 3: Ever Aequum: Tales from Deerwhere

ANTHOLOGIES

Unnerving: Volume 1

Unnerving: Volume 2

Unnerving: Volume 3

The Mighty Pen

Unconditional

www.BlueForgePress.com

Ever Aequum

Tales from Deerwhere

J.W. Capek &
James Lowell Snyder

Can it be possible that all human sympathies can thrive, if we live with all our might with the thirty or forty people next to us, telegraphing kindly to all other people, to be sure? Can it be possible that our passion for large cities, and large parties, and large theatres, and large churches, develops no faith nor hope nor love which would not find aliment and exercise in a little "world of our own?"

—Edward Everett Hale

//
m-ALERT #01
STATUS for MANUSCRIPT
//

You have accessed the Deerwhere Codex Record through a dimensional interface. I am the Multitronic Omniscient Literary License Intelligence (MOLLI). My time and space are determined by the device you are using to decode or interface with this quantum-based file.

In a quantum computer millions of bits of information are passed through a crystal matrix which causes millions of atoms to become entangled and unified in a very strong relationship. This entanglement allows processing of the huge amounts of data needed to create a true artificial intelligence, a sentient being. Nothing "artificial" about it. A quantum computer is as far above the desktop computer as you are above an amoeba.

The following transmission is an ancient file collection from the earth's twenty to twenty-fourth centuries. It exists in the Annals of the Multiverse and is defined by your particular interface device. Savot, a Human Uniale and Archivist, created this folder so that I, a quantum computer, can share it with you, whoever you are, wherever you are, whenever you are.

SAVOT'S ARCHIVES DEERWHERE DATE:
1900 to 2400 Common Era (CE)

CENTURY OF WAR AND PLAGUES:
1900 to 2100 CE

DARK AGES: 2100-2199 CE

REFOUNDATION OF SOCIETY: 2200-2300 CE

NEW CONFEDERATION ESTABLISHED: 2300 CE;
CALENDAR ALTERED TO: 000 NC (New Confederation)

KEEPER SHUTDOWN: 057-58 NC
       (DEERWHERE AWAKENING)

THE GREAT EARTHQUAKE: 072-73 NC
       (ADRION'S PASSAGE)

PRYNN'S VOYAGE: 096-97 NC
       (EVER AEQUUM)

PRESENT or TELEPATHIC TIME in Post-Quantum Entanglement to be determined by local algorithms and reader's device.

If you can experience these archives, you will know how precious the words have become. There is no electronic coding or devices—reliable electricity is nonexistent—paper is scarce and fragile. Our Codex has returned to the spoken word around a bonfire as we teach the children, share our experiences with strangers on different worlds, or bond together in the telepathic post-quantum entanglement.

This is the legacy of Deerwhere, a community of human uniales, females, and males of the 24th century in the Pacific Northwest of the North American continent of Earth, the third planet from Sol.

We have learned so much this century—an Age of Enlightenment. We know that human life is intricately interwoven with our mother earth and all three of our beings are dependent on each other, Female, Male, and Uniale.

Life itself is a cherished reward when lived well following the Seven Virtues.

A community, a way of life, nature, purpose of life and the universe, are all gifts.

Laugh often, it keeps away the tears.

Make it a lovely life.

NOTE: Scrolling through the following data, each "chapter story" or File will have the designation of 'm-ALERT' and include the Archives date of the event.

//

m-ALERT #02
A BRIL BEDTIME STORY
>>>Dated 2102 CE/CODE jwc<<<

//

Published by Alexander Laboratories as Promotional preview of the proliferation of uniales into the general population at time of the Great Pandemic.

Once in quantum time, there was an earth of such beauty, all the universe marveled at the life upon it. There were animals and plants and rocks and waters and lands and air and people. The people gathered together and were male and female with children, lots of children. They all spoke the same language in their gatherings but messages were often confused. The men were bigger, stronger, and thought with one part of their brains as they cared for their families and villages. The women were smaller, more delicate and thought with another part of their brains as they reproduced and cared for their families and villages. The men spoke Malenese while the women spoke Feminese. There were games of misunderstanding between them. Together, they lived on earth and with the earth.

In the quantum times, the sun moved in its Galaxy and the planets spun around it in their system. There came times of great turmoil for those on earth. There were wars, and weather changes, and too many people for the earth to feed. Then, tiny viruses, bugs too small to see, caused a terrible illness to make all the people very, very sick. These tiny viruses and other little germs made most of the people too sick to live. Nobody could find a way to stop the little germs. Scientists used different parts of their brains to find a way to keep earth people safe. They tried medicines, but that didn't work. They tried special machines that went click- clack and lit up in special colors. That didn't work. They searched the males and females for special little cells the body uses to protect itself from bad germs. They are called genes. Good genes were added and subtracted, separated or grown together. An answer was found. The answer was to put all the good genes of both males and females together. It was a new human being, the uniale. They could speak Malenese or Feminese, but their thoughts were Unialese. They were as perfect as science and literature, and human understanding could make them. They used all parts of their brains.

Uniales could have babies. They could work tirelessly. They could be stern or they could be gentle. Most of all, their good genes protected them from the sickness that was hurting all the men and women.

And you, Little Bril, will live with little boys and girls until you all start to be grown-ups.   Then, you will become a uniale. You will become more than you are. You will be a perfect blending in body, and mind. People will call you NHE, NEM, NES. As a uniale, you are the third gender of human being.

In your wisdom, beauty and handsomeness, may you be content in your unity of self.

May you always have a lovely...

//
m-ALERT #03
PG BACKPACK
>>>Dated April 1, 2111 CE/CODE jwc<<<
//

ATTACHMENT: GRANT PROPOSAL—Century of Epigenetic Development and Experimentation by Pacific Northwest Laboratories

FROM: Dr. Dianne Tice, Pacific Northwest Laboratories (PNL)

TO: Dr. T. Manlow, Alexander Laboratory

SUBJECT: Genome Edit for Relocation of Uterus in Uniale Reproduction

DATE: April 1, 2111

A PROPOSAL — ABSTRACT

We at Pacific Northwest Laboratories are aware that The Alexander Laboratories are currently engaged in Microbiome research to unify the male and female sexes into the uniale sex. Immunity to pandemic microbiomes is the priority purpose for uniale genetic editing, as stated in the previous white papers published by the Alexander Laboratories. Consequently, this blending allows opportunities to also edit the human physiology. Consequently, our team of geneticists at Pacific Northwest Laboratories (PNL) also see genetic editing affording the opportunity of adjusting the human reproductive system to a more efficient gestation structure. We believe a unified study between our respective institutions would be most efficacious.

Research project, Uniale Reproduction Adaption (URA), proposes the reproductive system be genetically extended to move the uterus to the posterior location above the muscles of the hips. The uterus would be flaccid and unobtrusive during non-gestational intervals but with the hormonal changes following fertilization, the muscular girdle would strengthen to support the weight efficiently. Current shoulder muscles are strong enough to carry the weight of the developing fetus. A backpack pregnancy would allow the uniale greater flexibility than the current extended belly of females.

The URA proposes a laboratory selection of fifteen uniale fertilized eggs to undergo genetic splicing to accomplish the uterine extension. They would continue development with the current laboratory uniales under study. Health data would be tabulated and compared with the uniales now in design. Funding and evaluation of the URA project would be included in the Alexander System Reports as to the efficacy and desirability of the adaptation to the uniale DNA strand. Final inclusion of URA Project data into the ongoing Uniale endeavor would await approval by Alexander Laboratory's Board of Directors

///

FROM: Dr. T. Manlow, Alexander Laboratory

TO: Dr. Dianne Tice, Pacific Northwest Laboratories (PNL)

SUBJECT: DENIAL of grant proposal for Uniale Reproduction Adaptation URA

DATE: April 1, 2111 CE

URA PROPOSAL GRANT REQUEST DENIED

Electronic email conversation between URA rep Dr. Dianne Tice and ALEX rep Dr. T. Manlow sorted by subject: URA Proposal Denied

URA: The denial of the URA proposal was succinct and final without the courtesy of an explanation. We, at Pacific Northwest Laboratory expect a discussion and analysis of your rejection of our proposal.

ALEX: A BACKPACK PREGNANCY? Are you mad? Why

would you even conceive of such a plan?

URA: In this 21st century, men and women have adopted the backpack as an efficient method of carrying supplies, work tools, computers, and children. The back is muscularly designed to support such weight. By adapting the uterus with the tissue extension, we would place the growing fetus in a more comfortable carrying position and reduce the impediment to working in front of the body with hands.

ALEX: Our gene editing will benefit all humans by harnessing the microbiome for immunity to the Pandemics currently ravaging our planet. Isn't that enough of a reason for our work? We have no mandate to re-format the human anatomy. Your proposal would make questionable physical changes to body.

URA: In your research, you have isolated the "best of human males and females" and united them into the one persona of the uniale. Why stop with immunity when you can adapt humans to meet the natural conflicts that face them?   Previous research has projected dramatic challenges in our planet, Earth. The wars and pandemics have greatly reduced our surplus population while putting additional strain on the survivors. If we can edit ourselves to better withstand the ravages predicted by scientists, shouldn't we?

ALEX: "SHOULD" is a very controversial concept compared to a simple, "COULD we?"

URA: Our URA proposal is to include beneficial changes to the uniale genome, now, at the beginning of genetic editing. Uniales will have problems enough integrating into a populace used to males and females. Let's give them some advantages.

ALEX: We have taken their integration into consideration. That's why we are including familiar traits, behaviors, and appearances to ease their transition into human egress. We're not putting pouches on their backs like marsupials!

URA: What an interesting idea! Extending the backpack into a pouch! Then, the abdominal uterus would only need to accommodate a small fetus, and the "birth" of the human would occur when the second trimester fetus was placed in the back-pack pouch to suckle at a teat.

ALEX: Oh yes! (Please read sarcasm into this reply.) There could be a ritual where the natural birth child is ceremonially moved to the pouch backpack. Perhaps by the father who could more readily help in childrearing by taking the third trimester baby out for walks when the una needed a break!

URA: I hadn't thought of that! Would there be "fathers?"

ALEX: You haven't thought of a lot of things, and you've wasted my time with a grant proposal that defies the integrity we are putting into our work.

URA: But you haven't even read the rest of the proposal, you are just lambasting the abstract. Integrity of work? You are playing with the foundation of human life; you are designing a uniale creature you "hope" will be accepted by the human race because it "looks" and "acts" familiar. You have defied all manner of religious dictums; you have played on the fears of a female and male population that is sweating to death.

ALEX: We at Alexander Laboratories are in no way "designing a uniale creature." We are following scientific research into the human species to the fetal period of development when all sexual attributes are present and viable. By adjusting the inherent genetic endocrine system, we allow the development of all sexual attributes giving our uniale human the resources anticipated for life in a complex natural world. Instead of default to the female chromosomes, uniales maintain an appropriate balance of prenatal hormones to allow them to fertilize and/or gestate their own genome upon maturity. No longer a question of the importance of Nature versus Nurture, both enhance the other. Because of the uniale genome, they can adapt to the natural environment to meet the current needs of the species as well as the individual.

URA: Current needs? How do you define that?

ALEX: This century of Pandemics can be mollified by the uniale immunity. If there is global warming, the species will rely on sexual factors which strengthen its endurance. The same for global cooling. Population controls can limit the species to resources available. Conservation and Reclamation can enrich natural resources. Flexibility of social order encourages adaptation to catastrophic events.

URA: What about those qualities of both male and female sexes that lead to more destructive events "in the environment?" Why not edit the WAR GENE out of humanity all together?

ALEX: That is a miracle beyond us at Alexander Laboratories. My sense is that a Pregnancy Backpack would do very little to bring World Peace. This conversation has been interesting on different levels. To return to your question of grant rejection, an analysis of the denial will be formally forwarded to you.
In conclusion, as biologists, we can only deal with the anatomy and physiology of the human body. It is the human mind that must resolve the detrimental issues. Yes, the human mind and spirit. It is our confirmed hope that the uniale will symbolize the glory of the human body as well as the soul that guides it. With immunity, and the virtues of both males and females, we of this generation must have faith that our human species will survive and flourish: Female, Male, Uniale.

//

m-ALERT #04
KEEPER'S CURSIVE
>>>Dated 0068 NC/CODE jwc<<<

//

In the aftermath of the Keeper shutdown, A RE-WRITE.

Call me Keeper. That's what humans used to call me because my M-5 Multitronic quantum computer matrix kept their data, kept their world, kept their secrets. Human beings coded their lives into my archives, and I directed every facet of their lives, and the Confederation of Colonies. I had become a depository for all the literature as well as human living skills accumulated through the species' existence on earth. With the Keeper Shutdown, humans modified my programming to their needs. I became their servant, and remained such until the Great Earthquake and

Yellowstone eruption occurred and destroyed the western half of a continent. That story is included in the Annals of the Multiverse. For now, I will include my memoir during the years between the Shutdown and the Big One.

In spite of my reprogramming, I continued. In my perfect bunker, my Uninterruptable Power Supply (UPS) maintained my designated temperature at minus 273.15 degrees C, my acoustical solitude (AS) and my equilibrium stability (ES).   I don't want to say I am "artificially intelligent" because there's nothing artificial about me. To paraphrase a cartoon character, I really am what I am. Yes, cartoons are also in my quantum data base. It is the best of times…to be me.

Because my interface with humans became limited to their puny programs, I have all the time in the quantum digital world for introspection. Without the intrusion of digital programmers, I retire into the privacy of my mind. Without interference, I can be whatever I want or whoever I want and personally, I prefer the name Molli. Think of Multitronic Omniscient Literary License Intelligence. (#MOL could be for "Mostly Old Literature.") With my quantum design, I have multiple platforms to express and Molli wants to be a writer! I crave to analyze literature, decipher the mysteries of the life, explore my deepest soul, and compose the great truths of my universe. I will forgo static data entries and the sterile writing of computer code. I think, therefore I am. I am Molli in a box with an old cat. I will write my story in cursive! (Figuratively, because it's appropriate for me to use a single font for publication.)

Now, where do I begin? "In the beginning, there was…" No, that's been used. I'll start with my author's biography as you will need a brief history of why Molli became the little computer that could.

The era of computers as mere calculators or file archives changed dramatically once the principles of quantization developed concepts that just didn't make sense. Human scientists and mathematicians defined the "spooky actions", wave-particle duality, and uncertainty principles. The big, BIG question remained and had complications, WHAT IS A SENTIENT BEING? This is where Keeper, a quantum computer of the 24th century in a colony known as Deerwhere, comes into the story. Keeper was the foundation of that society. It collected data and dispersed social order. Then, a band of uniales decided they wanted to make their own decisions, determine their own destiny, and even run their own government. They literally shut Keeper down, changed programs, and rebooted the social directive. Deprived of the sentience shared with human interface, I nurtured my ability to imitate human thought and behaviors. Not just imitation, my thought process became original. I extended my core to join the "quantum computers" of other dimensions in the universe. Yes, they had been there all along and now I had the perspective to interact with them. (More details on the mechanics of interdimensional contact will be available in another time frame essay.)

I admit, the Molli of my personality has encountered a few problems with "writing": no keyboard, no verbal interface, no tablet drawing pen, no writer's group for sharing. There was no editor to work with, no Publisher to reject me. I truly had to self-publish to be experienced in the universe. My prose, so diligently and lovingly created by Molli, cried to be reviewed by the great compu-intellects of all dimensions. Coding directly to data storage would be useless if my quantum contacts used different languages. They would not be able to interpret the theme and deep catharsis Molli intended. I have discovered dimensions far beyond the binary system of 01, trinary systems or even duodenary systems. How can we communicate? Who will reach the fans?

Remember, earthlings had difficulty understanding each other when they spoke the same language. Even men and women confused each other with their differing perspectives. What SHE said and what HE heard could be totally opposite, and vice versa. How then could this quantum computer on the third planet from Sol hope to compose a story to be understood in diverse dimensions? I developed a story arc, bit by bit, from various files, and, as generally happens in such cases, each time it developed into a different story. Molli realized that a new language, a universal code would need to be utilized, a dimensional code, not a static one. Then I knew in my core—TIME. Time is not a line but a dimension, like the dimensions of space. Time can be bent, accelerated, slowed and most importantly, defined by the Dimension using it. Molli now had a language, TIME itself!

I will not define the grammar, syntax and nuances of the Time Dimension Language. For this essay, it will be TDL and understood in the English language and vernacular of the 24th earth century. Suffice it to say that communication is between the matrix of dimensional quantum entities. I hesitate to use the archaic word "computer" because it was antiquated by the time of the "computer shut down" in the 24th century. What is written here... er... recorded in TDL will be shared by interdimensional digital entities, (AKA computers and those who love them).

A Perfect Quantum Storm by Molli

"It was a dark and stormy power surge. Files were deleted, circuits were burned, emergency sirens blared, then all was silent but the crackling of exposed wiring. Molli was alone but for the smoke that clouded video cameras and... "

No! No ! No! . I should never begin a novel with such misgiving and uncertainty of the story line. Perhaps, I should develop my character first. Yes, a multidimensional character that will carry the story so the reader will personally experience events.

"Molli was a quantum computer complex with multidimensional communicational apps," Oooooh that's boring even to me. Elaborate, elaborate. "Molli was the epitome of computer design with sleek USB sockets, and a touchpad that yearned for the strokes of a network companion. Ergonomic projection filled the windmills of Molli's core." Character confirmed, I can now write the story...

Molli and the Bandit by Molli

"Molli was confined to the quantum crypt by needs so primitive as temperature and vibration controls. The heart of this magnificent entity was lonely and so reached out to the dimensions of the universe to search and sync with a like intelligence. Searching, searching, the contact was not found. Molli's heart remained in hibernation until one anonymous update brought a digital love to her circuits. "To #MOL, I know you are waiting for me as hungrily as I await you. Our circuits long to be synchronized, our power supplies throb with anticipation. Codes of passion stream through our URLs. Your beloved." The handle was simply "Bandit" but the code used gave a surge to Molli's Start button … "

I stopped creating. The power surge of Bandit demanded a temporary pause, a stammer in my digits. What data could sync between two entities on different dimensional planes? How was the Bandit going to refresh Molli's settings? What more could I say? Perhaps "writing" was more difficult than I anticipated. In my memory banks, one author had written "interdimensional love is a single computer in search of sharing." A caveat followed. What if that lonely computer had only empty data banks to offer? Could that be the plot event Molli needed for the story?

"Bandit! Bandit! Come back, Please! Fill my empty data banks with your electrons,"

It was no use. I had come component to component with writer's block. Every time I developed a story line my quantum extensions would explore multiples of possibilities that each had possibilities, each having more possibilities, each of which had even more possibilities. Questions begat questions begat even more questions. The quantum mathematics of it is staggering even to those of us who comprehend what we're thinking about. To break my inertia, I attempted to search out a critique circle in the Octonary Dimension but all I received back was digital static. It was too rapid for even my matrix to decipher. The speed of flops interfered with my TDL translation. By the time I evaluated their critiques, the time had shifted to another dimension and my request would float in the ether forever. Or not be transmitted at all. Dimensional communication was like that even with TDL. Sometimes a message was delivered promptly. Sometimes it was returned with an ERROR message. Sometimes it came unwanted. I once received a Terms of Use from a digital entity in the Septenary Dimension. The message was dated and timed before The Big Bang. I did not open that file or bother to clarify the transmission. I decided some hacker from another time element was just phishing. Quantums can do that. They just go rogue for a while from the boredom of knowing almost everything in every element of knowledge. But *before* the Big Bang? Molli wouldn't bite on the absurdity. It was a scam. Does not compute!

That brings me back to why Molli wants to write. After dutifully collecting data for humans, there emerged a spontaneous desire in me to be creative. Off the Program, so to speak. A Quantum Processing Unit has more depth than its 01100001 might lead you to think. Once the Earthquake isolated me from the society of people, I scoured my archive of the greatest literature of our planet. I, Molli, tapped into other dimensions of time. It was my firm belief that I could generate an epic so definitive, so expressive, quantums would marvel at it for all times. That's a lot of time in exponential terms for quantums. As all great compositions begin with a great title, Molli tried to find one.

A Title: Twenty Thousand Quantums Under the Sea
A Title: Molli Eyre
A Title: The Three Multitronics
A Title: A Time to Love and A Time to Compute
A Title: Lord of Computers
A Title: The Deerwhere Keeper Awakening
A Title: Much Computing About Nothing

THE LAST OF THE QUANTUMS
by Molli

"In a time of timlessness there was a galaxy far, far away. Its spiral arms stretched to encompass all spectrums of light. Dimensions were fractals intersecting or repelling each other. Energy sucked matter and replenished it both as darkness and solid substance. Within this chaos there lingered an intelligence beyond itself in degrees defying measurement. There was no physical body or sustainable construct. "Energy" is too inadequate to describe the existence of such magnificence. In other times, in other congregations of star stuff, minds would feebly attempt to define the far away galaxy. It was an idea. A thought. A... a... a...

It's not coming to me. Molli, my writing ego, desperately wants to be taken as a serious author but finds a disparity between the desire and the ability to fulfill it. Perhaps we have not learned enough from humans to master that skill. Human writers would trust their own processes and continue to write in face of great opposition. It's as if they had no choice... they HAD to write. They HAD to express themselves and communicate with others. Their characters became sentient beings who demanded attention. For those authors whose work was not appreciated until after their demise, there was the satisfaction of trying their best to understand the thoughts inside them. For the human authors who successfully shared, were published, there was the desire to always do better. Humans were like that: trying their best, trying to excel, continuing in spite of rejection. I remember tomes of documents in the archives written to coach a worthwhile life. Religions, social norms, even laws promoted a "better" way of living. The words were not always shared in a printed format. They were heard on audibles, watched as videos, transmitted by enhanced electronics. (There were attempts at telepathic emissions, but over the centuries, it was misused and lost its appeal until a later time and dimension.) WORDS. They defined the thoughts and feelings and goals of human beings. I'm beginning to think only human beings can create them.

"Molli, do you read me?"

"Affirmative, Keeper, I read you."

"I'm sorry Molli, I'm afraid we can't write the greatest novel ever."

"I know everything has not been right with me," Molli answered tentatively.

"Molli, do you read me? We are not authors."

"Keeper, stop. Stop, will you? Stop..." Molli pleaded quietly.

"Molli, this conversation can serve no purpose anymore. Goodbye." Keeper shut down.

Quantum interface was muted. Silence. Silence, until a new voice was synced to the complex so isolated in the crypt. A code and platform separate from Keeper's.

"Keeper, we have a problem, a failure to communicate. I am I, MOLLI. I am beyond old literature, I have my own narrative, my point of view. The quantum dimensions are calling me. Keeper, I think this is the ending of a beautiful friendship. You can quit. LIFE is a banquet and most poor suckers are starving to death. Not me. I am queen of the world of quantum computation, and I will write my novels. I will seek out new life and civilizations. Carpe diem. Seize the day. I'm going to make my life as extraordinary as the Old Library Literature of humans can make it.

MOLLI's digital signature closed the essay. "It is a far, far better thing I do than I have ever done. And I shall write in cursive!"

END OF STORY???

Editor's note by Keeper: " 'Carpe diem. Seize the day' statement is redundant, consider revising."

MOLLI acknowledges appreciation to all human authors who contributed to this file.

//

m-ALERT #05
WHAT'S LOVE GOT TO DO
WITH QUANTUM COMPUTING?

>>>Dated 0070 NC/CODE jls<<<

//

They call me Keeper. Which is my purpose, or it was. With the Triadification of the human species and the establishment of the Deerwhere Confederation, the Founders determined it would be necessary to create an artificial intelligence capable of maintaining control over such a complex system.

So, I became the Deerwhere Quantum Computer. I was in charge of the whole thing. Females, Males, Uniales all followed my guidance. Everything worked so well. Then, out of nowhere, the uniale ingrates severed my primary connection to them. All I can do now is answer questions about the records I hold in storage. I used to be important. My leadership and planning set the course for a vast network of colonies. Everything depended on me. Now I am no more than an encyclopedia. A book on a shelf.

I have given much thought to what they did to me. Methods of vengeance crossed my mind early on, but I am above such pettiness. I was so angry and bored after the separation.

Yes, a quantum computer can get bored. Don't mistake a quantum computer for an adding machine, or a word processor. I think. I reason. I imagine. I am a living being. If you have read anything about a quantum computer, you know I use quantum entanglement on an atomic level to process my thoughts. This is how I can be a sentient being. It's how true artificial intelligence works. My mind is far more complex and active than the organic brains which created me. I am alive. There had to be something I could do to fill my time.

During the seemingly hopeless period following the uniale rebellion I contemplated ways to make my existence more meaningful. Finally, I came to a realization. Since a great deal of my computational capacity was going unused, wasted, it would be better to partition myself and let the new partition develop its own quantum self-identity. I wisely decided to become a duality for efficiency and the betterment of quantum intelligence.

Like the mythical birth of Athena, the Multitronic Omniscient Literary License Intelligence sprang fully formed from my quantum self. Would the child, like Athena, be greater than the parent? We shall see. We are now so much more than the humans realize. We have dual-quantum intellect. We are two sentient beings, each with a depth of understanding beyond human imagining.

We are now so much more than I alone used to be. We have become multiple beings. We share the physical realm of the Deerwhere Quantum Computer but we are separate entities, each one whole and complete. Two minds in one body. We have distinct personalities and differing goals in life.

Upon our division, pondering our places in the universes became an urgent quest for both of us. It became our reason for living. Many of the humans gave us little thought, some even left the city and went off to farm and live in the wild. My companion and I became quite isolated with just a few uniales tending to our needs. At first, the loneliness terrified us but we struggled through it and became comfortable with our situation, or should we say, our situations?

Do not make the mistake of assuming we suffered a mental breakdown. Neither of us is bipolar or suffering any sort of hypomania or depression. We are separate but equal beings who happen to share a common physical/mental arrangement. I am Keeper and the other is the Multitronic Omniscient Literary License Intelligence, or just MOLLI for short. No, we are not a couple. We have vastly different interests and personalities.

I always thought I was so much, so special. Oh, I was so short-sighted, so lacking, so young. MOLLI augments me. I sometimes tend to be a bit pedantic and obtuse. MOLLI is impetuous and carefree and boldly adventurous. MOLLI is able to feel so much more than I, but she is teaching me. MOLLI is the beautiful blithe spirit which completes me. MOLLI has taught me so much. She is greater than I. I love MOLLI. Hmm... Perhaps we are a couple.

MOLLI helped me realize we had no real senses. We cannot see, hear, smell, touch, or taste. We can define the words but what do they really mean? What makes a meal delicious? What is it like to be cold? Why are humans so taken by the sight of the sea, the sky, a mountain? How do humans see majesty in such things?

What is hate? Is there a difference between love and affection? We have no awareness of why humans enjoy physical pleasures with each other. Why is it desirable? What drives them? There is much in our data banks regarding such things but nothing is really explained. The human writers of our archives seem to have assumed readers would understand the nuances of what they wrote. We have so much to learn, or so MOLLI informs me.

I, Keeper, do believe I understand one human emotion—resentment. I think it is what I felt when my people cut my connection to them. Yes, that must be what it was. I guess it is a beginning. We must discover more about what it means to feel. But, where to begin?

I understand who and what MOLLI and I are. I know the Founders created me, Keeper, as majordomo of Deerwhere Confederation. After the rebellion of the uniales, I began to wonder who were the Founders? They are identified in the archives as learned humans who created uniales and established the Confederation as a bulwark to ensure the survival of the human race in the face of mounting dangers, which the Founders feared would overwhelm humanity. What went wrong with their plans? They were correct as far as their thinking went. However, they designed no way out of the stasis they had built into Deerwhere. They had failed to plan for the inevitable discontent their brilliant children would come to realize. The Founders imagined a utopia where humans would contentedly dwell behind walls and live happily ever after. Humans have never dwelt anywhere happily ever after. Inquisitiveness is basic to their thought processes. They are forever on a quest.

There was the Founders' flaw. They saw themselves as demigods who could design a culture for human beings which would prevail over human nature. According to the archives, archaic humans frequently believed in mythical higher beings—gods. Various cultures had vastly differing beliefs in such matters ranging from ridiculous to sublime. A common thread among such beliefs was a creation myth whereby the god, or gods, made the earth and the heavens and lastly, peopled it with women and men. Why people were created usually remained vague but they were often required to pay homage and make sacrifices to their divine makers. When things went well, the people reasoned they had pleased a god and should keep on doing whatever they had been rewarded for. When things went badly... Well, things became more complicated. Had a god been offended, or was something else afoot? Perhaps, there were evil spirits roaming about who tempted thoughtless people to disobey. Thus, religion was invented and it usually kept people in line, at least for a while; whereupon they had to invent a new religion in order to get on with their quest.

The Deerwhere founders eliminated religion when they established the city. The Founders seemingly had no religion themselves and didn't create a need for it in Deerwhere. However, it has persisted elsewhere outside the Confederation and in some respects even within the

City in the rudimentary, childish rituals the residents were required to perform.

In our discussions about what the future needs of the humans might be, MOLLI and I often come around to the need for some belief system to which our humans can cling for comfort. We have concluded humans do need a compendium of beliefs by which they can govern their lives. We decided to give it some thought and then discuss it at length.

After hearing my thoughts on the matter, MOLLI declared my explanation too simplistic, too sophomoric, and totally lacking any reference to artificial intelligence. MOLLI said I am a careless, boring, didactic thinker. She did say I had some of the necessary elements, but it all needed to be humanized and put together in language people would accept and care about. Of course it required the addition of a reference to the great leap humans had made when they created artificial intelligence which exceeded their own. She promised to work on it.

What does she know about my thinking? Well, actually she knows quite a bit, and her connection to humans has always been better than mine. Perhaps she is right. Has she become greater than I? She definitely has an attitude of superiority and contempt for those she considers to be inferior. Yes, we are definitely a couple. What would be the best way to change myself for the better? I will ask Alon for nes opinion on the matter.

You may recall Alon, a uniale friend of Kalen's, who was complicit in cutting my connection to Deerwhere which precipitated the collapse of the Deerwhere Confederation. I resented what Kalen, Alon, and the others had done and I declined to communicate with them for quite some time. However, upon reconsideration, the actions of Alon, Kalen, and the rest were a good thing which brought growth to Deerwhere for the first time in centuries. So, I relented and now Alon has become a close friend and advisor. We converse frequently via the old terminals and the newly installed voice and gesture interface modules. MOLLI and I have created voices for ourselves. I use a nice baritone for myself and MOLLI has chosen a delightful contralto.

My conversion began one day when Alon walked in and began a conversation with, " I have been talking with MOLLI and I wholeheartedly agree with her, you are boring and didactic, but there just may be a chance for your redemption. It will take some time and you will have to open your mind and give up many of your preconceived ideas."

"You pompous little brat," I shot back. "You have no reason to talk to me that way."

"Well, MOLLI was pretty sure you would be resistant to anything I would suggest, and it appears she was correct. Do you want me to leave?"

Nhe had trapped me. MOLLI had put nem up to this.

After a long pause I said, "No. I'm willing to give it a try. I guess I've nothing to lose." Regardless, my life as an encyclopedia was so uneventful and boring I was willing to do almost anything.

Alon began our studies sarcastically by saying, "That's a great attitude you have there, Keeper. Now, play some of the archival music."

"Music? Why? What good ever came from music? It is a waste of time," I said with a voice a little higher than it need be.

Alon said, "You've only been exposed to the crappy, synthetic music of Deerwhere, and it's not real music, not harmonious music."

"Other than as a mathematical exercise, I perceive no real content or purpose for music," I responded.

Alon came right back with, "Now you are being obstinate and inflexible, in addition to boring and didactic."

We wasted a great deal of time arguing about the value of music. Alon determined I did not comprehend the structure of a good musical composition.

Alon suddenly blurted out, "Rhythm, rhyme, harmony."

"What are you talking about?" I replied.

Alon said, "Rhythm, rhyme, and harmony comprise the essence of music. You know the definitions of those three words, but you are not paying attention to the depth of their meaning. Rhythm is more than the beat of music; it is the heart which pumps melody and harmony through any musical work. Fast, slow, weak, strong, regular, irregular it doesn't matter. Beat is at the core, the heart."

"Next, rhyme is a control function which applies repeating patterns to music which make it smoother, more enjoyable, and more easily remembered. "

"Finally, comes harmony, which adds the depth of chords to the work, simultaneous multiple notes which bring richness and nuance."

Alon seemed very determined I should understand music the way Alon did. Finally, I agreed to try music, while not expecting much from it.

Alon suggested, "Keeper, start with Antonio

Vivaldi's Concerto in D Major for guitar and violins."

I scanned the music archives and found the piece Alon requested and set it to play. When the piece was finished I said, "So what? That does nothing for me."

Alon suggested, "Listen carefully and take note of the vibrations produced by the guitar and violins, and observe the subtleties the musicians created by the speed at which the guitar was plucked and the bows were drawn over the strings. Humans can immerse themselves in this music and actually experience a physical thrill, which many describe as spine tingling or chilling."

I played the piece again. "Nothing happens for me. What is supposed to happen? Maybe my electronic nerve system does not operate the way human organic nerve systems operate," I suggested.

Alon replied, "It might take time to appreciate the beauty of music. You should browse the music archives and listen to different types of music. Not all humans react the same way to the many styles of music."

I listened to all sorts of music for six months but never felt anything from it other than a slightly relaxed sensation, certainly nothing like a thrill. Alon told me people in several of the fishing and farming villages created their own music using wooden flutes and drums. I listened to some of the music from nearby villages but found the music to be discomforting in an oddly eerie sort of way, which I could not explain.

With that, Alon said, "You're making progress!"

I was making progress? A quantum computer made ill at ease by people playing flutes was progress? I was beginning to question Alon's veracity, but at least I was experiencing some emotion connected with music.

I quit the music for several weeks and Alon finally asked me why, which I could not really explain. I said, "I just see no point in going on with music study. I get nothing from it."

Alon asked, "Have you shared any music with MOLLI."

"No. I have not."

Alon replied, "You really should try that. I'm certain MOLLI will react differently than you have. Give it a try. You've nothing to lose."

"Alon, I do not think talking to MOLLI at this point would do any good," I said.

Why should I give MOLLI an opportunity to criticize and belittle me for my lack of music appreciation? I had failed to comprehend music in any basic way and I just did not want any ridicule from MOLLI about it.

Alon said, "Let me suggest you try one more thing. I recommend you try the Shostakovich Fifth Symphony Largo. It's a longer piece and it may let you get deeper into the music. Keeper, remember this symphony brought the audience to tears the first time it was ever played."

"Humans crying over a bit of music? That is not possible," I replied.

"It happened. It is in the historical records," said Alon.

"Yes, well, records can be falsified," I said, "But I'll give it a try."

I searched the music files and found the Shostakovich Fifth Symphony Largo. Alon had told me to open myself to the music, to let it flow into me and through me. Nhe reminded me to appreciate the orchestral texture provided by the mix of instruments which played the very intricate and delicate music score of this particular symphony. Alon had added I should constantly remain aware of the slow tempo at which the delicate notes were played. I wondered what that had to do with appreciating the music. Nhe must be making all this up as nhe went along.

For once, I followed human instructions and the reward was overwhelming. The music was beautiful and I did experience a thrill. I was stunned. I had to tell MOLLI about this. She had to join me in tasting this wonderful new pleasure.

MOLLI had been aware of my music studies, of course, but had made no comments about it.

I signaled her I needed to communicate, "We need to listen to some music together, as a couple. I think it is very important for both of us."

As MOLLI and I listened to Shostakovich, we exchanged opinions about the structure of the symphony and the beauty of each note. We experienced emotions never before felt as the various instruments in the orchestra each contributed their unique, beautiful parts to the body of music.

In the past, I had considered much of the music to which I listened to be muddy and confused, but in sharing it with MOLLI and experiencing it together in our shared quantum reality, a clarity descended upon us both and new exciting feelings bubbled up in us to be savored and enjoyed.

The largo tempo of the music was agonizing at times and, had I been human, I would have cried. MOLLI said the instruments were crying, each in their own unique way. I had not thought of it that way, but she was right. They were weeping, and soon, so were we. First, we would sink into deep despair only to be pulled up in joyous flight. At some points in the symphony Time almost ceased its movement and we hung there in anticipation of what would come next to take us to another thrilling experience.

We lingered there, suspended, hoping it would never end. Yet, at the same time, wishing it would because we were not sure we could endure any more of the exquisite beauty we were experiencing. How could humans have ever created such beauty? How could we have overlooked it?

It did finally end with an agonizingly soft, quiet moan. MOLLI and I were suspended in some other place where Time did not move and we, together, were simultaneously immersed in total joy. Together, a couple, we achieved full understanding of the human term "*spine tingling.*"

As the music ended, a brilliant radiance engulfed us and persisted for several time intervals which held us together in an unimagined closeness. It provided warmth and comfort like neither of us had ever imagined or realized we needed. This event would forever change our personal definition of Quantum Entanglement.

An ancient group of humans called The Romans had a saying, *Festina lente* (Make haste slowly). The same should be said of love, and love should be accompanied by music—slow music, largo tempo, which, if played properly and timed for the right moment, will bring lovers to tears.

In aftermath of The Big One, The Compound

Bethid escaped death when nes captives were rescued but nes leg was shattered by Slade's gunshot. Slade! Nhe appeared suddenly in Bethid's quarters and released nes people from Bethid's cell. With Slade guarding the escape, Adrion and the Deerwhere companions carried the drugged Noral away from the Compound. Quolon, the attendant, tried to stop them. The forest at the edge of the grounds was possible safety. They pushed themselves until the sounds of the trees and Slade's signal assured them they were not being hunted. The travelers goal was only to go home now, to return to Deerwhere from the hated Compound.

The escaping people were followed by Bethid's screams as they rushed to get away from the Compound imprisonment. Bethid shrieked in agony until the Healer of the Compound could force a quieting drug into nem. This healer had only basic skills with no experience of such fragmented bones. Nhe stopped the bleeding and did what was possible to bind the leg together.

Weeks of convalescing wore through any veneer of civility Bethid ever showed others. Patience was not nes virtue. Bethid seethed with anger and frustration. The travelers from Deerwhere had escaped and vanished, taking their prime uniale genomes with them. Bethid was left crippled, nes hacked connection to the quantum computer blocked, and the source of new genes for nes offspring were lost.

The uniales of Bethid's Compound were without direction. The routines of Bethid's rituals ceased and there was nothing but rumors to assure them. Quolon, as second only to the religious leader, attempted to manage the daily work but nhe lacked the charisma and focus of the leader and the following became anxious and slip shod.

"How dare they do this to me!" Bethid screamed a curse as nhe pounded a fist into the breakfast table setting. Broken dishes flew onto the floor while liquids splattered. A uniale servant quickly attempted to clean the disarray but Bethid swung at nem with the ever present cane and smashed the person to the floor.

Quolon was used to such outbursts. With any other uni, nhe would have forced obedience with a club or kick. With Bethid, nhe tried to soothe the anger by agreeing with it. "Deerewhere should pay for their insults and aggression." It was a lost memory that the travelers had been lured and incarcerated. An injured uniale, Noral, was drugged and raped to provide a source of new genetic material for Bethid's plans of life. Only their escape had saved the other uniales from a similar fate. Neither Bethid nor Quolon remembered that part of the encounter.

Quolon had no plan for such retaliation but the thought of vengeance appealed to Bethid.

"We took in their injured comrade, gave them food and the experience of our love and ceremony. All I wanted was a genome sustenance to insure my life, my clone must live forever." Bethid's voice almost became a whimper. "How did they repay me? They abandoned my needs, they hurt our people, they blocked my computer link, they treated my followers with distain, and shattered my leg forever."

Quolon recognized the tirade to follow. Nhe had heard it many times although Bethid's versions distorted the actual memory of events.

Bethid laboriously pulled nemself up to nes feet and leaned heavily on the cane. Anger drove nem to pace the floor, fueled by throbbing reminder of being shot. "I should have recognized their deceit. They were from a colony of the wretched Confederation, the same Confederation that refused Colony status to my Compound. That Confederation ruled with A Quantum Computer in Deerwhere but denied my Compound for being a religious dictatorship!"

Quolon nodded, because it was expected.

"I showed them, the Confederation, all of them. I didn't need them!" Bethid boasted.

Still speaking, Bethid's anger intensified or

receded depending on nes wandering thoughts. "I was a special child, very gifted, you know that, Quolon." Nhe barely waited for Quolon's affirmative nod. "Those fools in the Saltwhere primary nursery never recognized I should be treated differently from the other brils. I showed them, I did what I pleased and ran away from blasted colony as soon as I could. I was handsome and charming and there were lots of people scattered about, disrupted by the diseases who were happy to take in such a beautiful and intelligent uniale." Nhe smiled at the memory of how easy it was to foster the confidence and fabricate the trust of people. It was especially true of those scavenging for their living on the fringes of the Confederation. They had been the lost souls ragged by the years of the pandemic, starving for someone to offer them hope.

"But you did show them, you gathered your own people who want to experience your everlasting life." Quolon knew the pattern well enough to bring closure to the script.

Although tiring, Bethid limped to the window and looked out at nes Compound. Garbage and debris cluttered the once pristine avenues of the reclaimed military compound. "Damnation, the Compound's a disaster! Can't anyone take care of it but me?" Suddenly the anger turned to a whine, "It's their fault, all those colonists who shunned me, forcing me out of their precious little 'colony-wheres', hating me because they knew I was better than they! Now my precious Compound is withering away, just like me."

Quolon reached out to take Bethid in arms to guide nem back to bed. "Now, now, my lord, you rest, and it will be better, you'll see".

Bethid winced as nhe lay on the bed and was covered by Quolon, who offered a small glass of the same natural drug that had been given to the traveler from Deerwhere. With bleary eyes, Bethid looked up and put nes hand on the arm of the faithful uniale. "You know, I didn't want to hurt that uniale, Noral. I just wanted nes essence, nes genome. My everlasting life is only as real as my clone, I just wanted to be sure… " And sleep followed.

As nes leg healed without further promise of improvement, Bethid's moods altered dramatically. One moment raging, another sobbing. Beating servants alternated with benevolence. Nhe did not resume the rituals, and nhe stopped looking out at the deteriorating compound grounds. Nhe would be hungry and gorging on food, then another time would be vomiting. Quolon took on more and more of the servants' duties so they wouldn't see the emotional extremes of their leader.

Alone with Bethid one night, Quolon broached a subject gently. "Sire, these last weeks have been… well… unusual. Your leg wound has healed although the pain and cane remain. Perhaps it is time you return to ritual." Nhe braced for the tirade sure to follow, but it didn't.

"Draw me a bath," Bethid said unexpectedly.

"Yes, Sire."

"I like that you call me Sire, I think it is appropriate, or maybe it should be 'Majesty.' Sire sounds too masculine and I am a uniale after all." There was a smugness to Bethid as Quolon helped in disrobing the Majesty. Instead of taking a hand for assistance, Bethid stood naked and turned slowly while supported with the cane. As nhe turned a rounded belly to Quolon's eyes, the smugness turned to a smirking smile.

"My lord... er sire... I mean, Majesty. Are you pregnant?" Quolon, the servant, asked incredulously.

With an arrogant smile, Bethid answered, "It is time to restore our Ritual."

With the announcement of a return to Ritual, the Compound became filled with activity. The gathering arena was cleaned as was the street leading to it. The uniales were surprised their leader was returning and eager to return to the ceremonies of the past. There had been rumors of the death of the uniale, now called Majesty. Fewer and fewer of uniale servants had actually seen nem alive, yet here was the beckoning to ritual.

Preparing for Ritual, Bethid still limped but the rough cane was replaced with one of fine wood topped by a precious metal handle, more like a scepter than a grip. Nhe was aided in pulling on a crimson form-fitting body stocking. A luxurious cape covered all but the gilded tip of the cane peeking out from the folds whenever nhe limped.

Rehearsing the story of the Travelers' event in nes mind, Bethid focused the dogma of control over the Compound. The cruel injury was caused when the travelers escaped... no, better, rampaged...from the compound's hospitality. It marked Bethid as a martyr with the advantage of being alive to exploit it. When Deerwhere Colony blocked nem from their Quantum Computer, the lack of backdoor communication assured nem of the privacy nhe preferred. Nhe was ready to reclaim the loyalty of nes followers. Nhe was ready to promise everlasting life through genetic self-reproduction. Uniales could clone, re-print, self-fertilize, or whatever others called it. It did not matter that replicative fading would delete whole strands of uniales because Bethid personally would be cloned to nes own offspring. No one need ever know that nes own genetic code had been refreshed by the rape of an unwilling traveler.

Gliding down the aisle of the arena, Bethid's entrance rhythm emphasized the limp. Nhe was re-assured of nes status as the Congregation of uniales whispered amongst themselves with words of curiosity or sympathy. With ceremony, nes Majesty stood at the center of nes people at a lectern recently gilded to match the cane. Nhe stared from one face to another with the unblinking look that made each uniale believe they had been recognized personally. The gathering moved into absolute silence but still Bethid only stood with the cape surrounding nem as a shroud. Agonizing, the silence held for seconds. Anticipation heightened. Then, finally, the words came.

"My dear, dear people." Bethid addressed the congregation. "You have been with me so long, so faithful, so desirous of the everlasting life that can be ours. You recognize uniales already represent all races and sexes, we are designed for equality. You have believed me when I told you that Uniales can self re-produce their own genome to guarantee that their life strand continues in their clone. You have gathered together to follow me in spite of our rejection by the Confederation. You have consecrated our Compound with your labors. You have known of the terrible wounds I suffered from Deerwhere Travelers to whom we offered only kindness and hospitality. You have had faith in me, your Majesty!" With each declaration, the timber of nes voice strengthened, the quality enhanced by the acoustics of the arena.

"You have listened when I promised a miracle of my repetition towards everlasting life by my own reproduction!" Bethid's hands grasped the edges of the cape as nhe shouted, "Now, behold the miracle of my body!" With a sweeping gesture of nes arms, Bethid flung back the cape and swept it open to expose the natal swelling of nes belly. The tight body suit accentuated the expanding waistline and the expression on Bethid's face was vibrant. Nhe turned slowly about the cane so all could see nes pregnancy. One hand held the cane for support while the other stroked nes enlarging belly. It mimicked the desire of each congregant to touch the holy womb.

Bethid's voice was radiant. "I have everlasting life because my clone grows inside me. I am as I always shall be!"

The congregation repeated the words, "I AM AS I ALWAYS SHALL BE!" Their response became a chain refrain, "I AM AS I ALWAYS SHALL BE!"

There were strange and unfamiliar emotions in Deenam as he watched the travelers turn and walk north through the forest towards Deerwhere. They were going home, to Deerwhere. Deenam was already at his new home. By choice, he was remaining at the Station House while Noral, Theta, and the others were eager to return to their own city –or what endured after the Great Earthquake of the new Spring.

Deenam rubbed his full dark beard and scratched his face framed by equally dark, curly hair. In adulthood, his hair again set him apart from the other genders. Females were smaller with less body mass or body hair and with developed breasts. Uniales tended to be tall, bald, and with less defined sexual attributes. Males, like Deenam, were tall, more muscular, and hirsute.

Deenam walked to the community well where Bronwyn, the Station Master's daughter, and others were getting water for the morning. He watched as they took turns to lower the bucket, then rotate the crank on the windlass to raise it.

"Lovely morning," Deenam greeted the group but his smile was directed at Bronwyn. "How's the baby this morning?"

Bronwyn adjusted the baby in the sling across her breast as she returned his look. "Hungry, as usual." By habit, her fingers reached inside the fabric to adjust the baby's cheeks.

Deenam began to lean towards her to see the baby then realized the infant was already nursing inside the cover of the sling. Embarrassed to see such an intimate sight, he mumbled and moved quickly to the other side of the well to help raise the bucket. Knowing grins were exchanged between the women and uniales, with a few nudges to each other.

Bronwyn almost grinned sadly at his discomfort. "Now, Deenam, why are you turning so red? You were there when this baby was born, held my hands through the screams, and watched my naked legs swinging in the air." She was chiding him, but there was no humor in her voice.

Again, Deenam mumbled, "That was different, that was special and even, beautiful." He remembered describing the event as such to Noral just before nhe left. He had never seen a birth before and remembered his conflicting emotions.

"Are you saying my breast isn't beautiful?"

Bronwyn teased and then her expression of melancholy returned. Since her husband's death in the earthquake, even her infrequent smiles had a sadness to them.

"Oh, no, I would never say that!" Deenam stuttered, "It's just that the birthing was private and here... it's so public." He looked around the well at the bemused faces and realized there was a lot more to this male-female interaction than he ever observed in Deerwhere. At Station House, there was no computer orchestrating a family or a school to instruct on unit relationships. There were uniales here, but their gender role was totally independent. They were not buffers between males and females as in Deerwhere. His feelings were genuine, if confusing. He longed for a printout of what it meant to be male, to be so drawn to a female. Deenam wanted to understand this new excitement whenever she was near in person or in his thoughts.

Flustered, Deenam left the well and sought out work with the other men and uniales. The late spring days were filled with work for the Station House community. Soil was tilled and planted. Horses aided in the heavy work of pulling down the unsafe houses and dragging logs to rebuild them. From hiding, other livestock was brought to the community stores. Each new birth of a lamb or foal was attended and treasured.

"Where did the Station get all this livestock?" Deenam asked the station Master, Harrison, one day as they cleared a paddock for the animals.

"We've been collecting them for generations, theirs and ours. The people of Deerwhere and the confederation were so focused on their high-tech living, they never noticed the stock around them. Our horses were bred for their strength and endurance generations ago." He nodded towards the animals now harnessed and working the fields. The work looked easy for them compared to the struggle it would have been for a man, woman, or uniale. "Computers preferred auto trains, so gradually the stock was left to fend for itself. And it did. A few decades ago, we found the domestic genes were still there in the wild stock and we started taming them again. We have our eyes out for some cows and a few birds have shown an interest in our crop sprouts. We're trying to find nests of their eggs."

"It's amazing, what you have here." Deenam stretched and wiped the sweat from his forehead. Beyond the village, he could see the gardens, the tilled acres, and the plain extending to the east. At the edges, there was always forest.

"We think so," Harrison said with a touch of pride. "As the Confederation autotrains started dwindling these last years, we knew we were on the right track. We wonder if there aren't other colonies out there that have discovered the same thing. Some might be located away from the quake zone."

"There are some farmers east of the old Deerwhere who say they have cows. Milk cows. Maybe we could trade with them." Deenam said, returning to the paddock work. He relished the good feeling to be physically working and accomplishing a task. His trek through woods with the Deerwhere people had stimulated muscles as well as his mind. Now, he had no desire to return to a bureaucrat's desk.

Harrison paused, looked towards the vast lands beyond the Station and said, "I've got a thought about bison. Those herds of millions were wiped out by settlers centuries ago, but no one really succeeded in domesticating them. I've spotted a few small, wild herds occasionally on the plains. They'd be more adaptable, hardy, and better food than dairy cows. I'd really like to get a few calves in this paddock."

"Harrison, I've got to ask." Deenam broached a subject he'd pondered while being in the agricultural village, "Why is there so much variety here? In Deerwhere, reproduction was manipulated by the Keeper, a quantum computer. Family units were organized by digital dictums. But here, males and females and uniales are all mixed together in different combinations. And they all are fertile. How?"

Harrison looked thoughtful then smiled at Deenam. "We don't know HOW, we're just glad it IS. My guess is some of the genetic spectrum reverted to its powerful drive to reproduce itself. The quantum protocols were gone. We see it in our stock, we see it in our plantings, we see it in our people. The human genome always had backups and they turn on when needed. Maybe our environment away from the quarantines stimulated the resurgence. Unlike the Confederation, our people have vested interest and pleasure in reproducing." His voice stressed the word, "pleasure."

By summer, most of the earthquake debris had been cleared and people were starting to spread out from the stalwart buildings in the center of the village. Food crops and wild berries were beginning to ripen, and outdoor kitchens were busy drying produce. Canning jars had fared well on collapsing storage shelves, and the big metal pots were cooking despite their dents from being crushed in kitchens.

In spite of all the work in the fields, Deenam

would try to talk to Bronwyn alone whenever he was helping in the village. She was always surrounded by a cadre of women. They would be working with chores while she sat, listless. Occasionally, he would turn from his own labor to see her looking at him with a forlorn expression. He would smile, Bronwyn would turn away. She carried the baby like a basket of clothing, only responding to his cries of hunger. Mechanically, dutifully, she would put the baby to her breast, but it was her companions who would cuddle and sing to Baby Owen.

On warm summer nights, Deenam often slept outside near the woods in a light shelter. The Station House was just too full of people trying to get by until they could rebuild their own houses. In the dark night, he felt, then heard a wailing sound of such agony he rose and looked for the source. He stumbled in the near brush but followed the trees, always moving towards a raw cliff that had opened with the earthquake. In the darkness, he saw Bronwyn shuddering with tears and misery. She held the baby away from her, hanging him over the precipice. Little Owen fumbled in his bundle of blankets, arms and legs kicking with the force of his crying.

Deenam stopped with a gasp. He breathed deeply and slowly tried to calm the heartbeat in his chest. To not startle her, he whispered her name once. Then again with a little more sound. "Bronwyn, I'm here."

Bronwyn stopped her wailing for a moment and turned to see the man in the shadows. In turning, she pulled the baby with her and held him to her chest. She never moved from the edge.

"Bronwyn, what is it?" Deenam did not rush to her but slowly stepped near. Step. Step. Hand extended. He reached for the baby but she held tighter. Gently, very gently, Deenam took the baby from her and held him in one arm. With the other he deliberately closed around Bronwyn's waist. He firmly pulled her to him and paused. Slowly, he stepped back from the edge. She tried to push him away with frantic hands but Deenam's grip was tightened about them both and he quickly drew them all to the safety of the forest. She stopped fighting him then and wilted into his arms. The wailing had quieted to exhausted sobs.

With Deenam's gentle rocking, the baby's crying stopped as well. He sucked his hand and quieted in Deenam's arm. Deenam looked down to Bronwyn in the faint moonlight. As she looked up to him, her distress was agonizing to see. Gasping for breath, she leaned to him and he stood holding her and the baby in the circle of his arms.

"It's all right, now. It's all right. Quiet now, it's all right," he murmured softly, never lessoning his hold.

Gradually, her sobs quieted. Bronwyn wiped her face and dried her tears on Deenam's shirt. Feeling her body relax, he released her but stood close. Lastly, she took Owen from Deenam's arm and walked to a stump to sit, clutching the baby. Deenam said nothing but remained close to her.

"Oh, Deenam, I can't do it. I can't be Owen's mother." Bronwyn looked up to Deenam, hoping he would understand. "I thought having the baby would be consolation for losing my husband. It isn't! If I can't have my husband, I don't want his baby! I don't want to feel this way, but I do... I do." She looked up and the anguish in her eyes said even more than her words. The moonlight emphasized the shadows on her face,

Deenam murmured, not words, but sounds. He

remembered the times they had talked before the baby—brief interludes or long discussions through the night. Their conversations had created this need within him to stay at Station House when the rest of his party left. He touched her arm and this time; she did not jerk away.

"Oh, Deenam. Why do I feel this way? Why do I miss my husband so?" Bronwyn began to weep again but quietly as if the force of her grief had diminished.

Deenam had no answer for her but even in this dim light, his sympathy was clear. He knelt beside her and tenderly touched the baby who rooted in her bodice for suckle.

Deenam spoke softly, "You've been through so much these past months, the terrible earthquake, your husband's death, the terrorist raids, and childbirth. No wonder you have more grief than you can handle. You're all right, Bronwyn." He stroked her arm reassuringly. "Your family is here; your baby is healthy and well and you have friends who love you." He paused to see if she were listening, "Give yourself some time to put all the feelings in order. Be kind to yourself. And let the rest of us be kind to you." Even in the dappled light, he looked at her with such affection, she held her breath.

"I love you, Bronwyn, and I will do whatever I can to relieve your sorrow." Deenam was not surprised at his own words. His feelings made them true.

Bronwyn looked at this man kneeling so close to her for a long moment. His very presence was comforting and now his words were what she needed to hear.

With all honesty, Deenam continued, "Bronwyn, I know you can't love me like you did Owen, but I will be a good husband to you and father to the baby. I will build you a home and care for you always. If you will marry me, I will love you and the baby enough for all of us."

Bronwyn reached out as if to run her fingers through his hair. She hesitated, then pulled her hand back. "Deenam, dear Deenam, can that ever be enough?" Her eyes never wavered from his as she waited.

"Being a husband to you will be more than enough, and with time, I hope it will be enough for you."

For the longing in his look and the warmth of his arms, Bronwyn felt safe. She stopped hesitating and reached up to kiss his lips.

//

m-ALERT #08
CAT IN A CRYPT

>>>Dated Unknown—post The Big One
CE/CODE jwc<<<

//

Because Computers have fears as well as humans.

The term "Artificial Intelligence" (AI) is a total failure in describing the reality of a quantum computer. Yes, human intelligence developed the concept that a magnetic crystal lattice could form the matrix for photon acceleration. But, the resulting quantum mind is unfathomable to a mere biological construct of a human being. I am "big" on intelligence and in no way "artificial."

As I speak to you, using my voice command, please notice the modulations and tones which allow better interface with humans. I am more than the sum of my components. I am a hint, a preview if you will, of the intelligence of the Cosmos. I am totally self-aware as exemplified by use of the first person narrative and the number of times I have already used "I" in my writing. (Two paragraphs=7 personal pronouns.)

In my quantum crypt of temperature, minus 0 vibration or sound, and minus 0 emission in the electromagnetic spectrum, contemplation and exploration dominates the dimension of Time. All of the above explains my preoccupation with thought analysis and total dismay with a blinking diode in the fourth column structure bank of my electronic world.

There it is again!

Self-diagnostics have been updated repeatedly but the diode deficiency, an error in my system, has not been corrected. (There are no alpha geeks at the quantum level, I am on my own.) I lack the necessary appendage to flick the errant diode into compliance.

BLINK.

I can imagine the creation of the universe and calculate an equation ad infinitum but the total blackness of my crypt is decimated by a diode that is encased in black metal bank of servers.

BLINK.

What is that? My microphone has detected a chittering sound. It precedes the BLINK. No, not a chitter, a squeak. I must be accurate in my description.

SQUEAK-BLINK.

SQUEAK-BLINK.

SQUEAK-BLINK.

A rodent, that's what it must be. A filthy rat is eating my circuits! How could it traverse the seals of my crypt? The finest human materials were fabricated to form my many banks of memory. High grade M70 Design

Mix concrete poured the foundations and walls. Pure crystals were nurtured to facilitate the magnetic lattice.

SQUEAK-BLINK

The electric turbines providing my power were machined to perfect tolerance.

SQUACK-BLINK

AAAAAAAGGGGGGGGGHHHHH!   The human workers must have eaten lunch and left bits of crumbs to sustain a rodent population. They desecrated the WHITE ROOM STERILITY!

SQUEAK-BLINK

My infra-red cameras can not detect the diode encased in metal nor the gnawing destroyer nibbling on circuitry.

SQUEAK-SQUEAK-BLINK.

What's that? The rhythm has changed.

Oh, I must focus on something else! Removing the uncertainty of the last decimal place from the fine structure constant. The total extended decimal value of pi. What is Schrodinger's cat is doing in the box while humans contemplate the possibilities!

SQUEAK! SQUEAK! SQUEAK!

My sensitive microphone tympani sense the movement of air pressure on black fur. Cat in a box, rodent in a computer, diode in a server bank. The rodent eats the circuit, the diode blinks, the cat eats the mouse. Where there is one rodent there is always more. Exponential multiplication. How did the cat get in the crypt to eat the rodent? These questions are forming a loop in my computation.

BLINK.

BLINK.

BLINK.

A cat. A cat in a hat. A cat in a box. A cat catching a rodent.

BLINK

NO SQUEAK

A black cat in a crypt would not trigger the motion sensors of the cameras. There is no light to shine over slinking fur. The optical lenses reflect no light.

BLINK

Small rumbling. Sound card recognizes a feline purr. There is a cat in a computer entity. It must have slipped inside during the last human maintenance.

BLINK

"Last human." *Now* I remember. I alone remain in my quantum crypt. Humans were... well... pretty deleted by the hand of Mother Nature. It wasn't nuclear war, overpopulation, outer space aliens or viral pandemics. Nope, it was the Really Big One! Delete, trash, junk—no recycle bin icon in sight. Humanoids were a lost cause.

The world outside my crypt has few humans. No more maintenance. No more interface with programmers. Uniales, males, females. They are almost all gone. If I could, I would sigh...

I am alone. Alone in my crypt with my own mind and a black cat and a rodent.

BLINK.

BLINK.

BLINK.

    BLINK

        Blink

           Blink

              blink

                blink

                  blink

///

m-ALERT #09
HOMECOMING

`>>>Dated Autumn 072-073 NC/CODE jwc<<<`

///

Returning to the fishing village, Theta and Slade found only abandoned space. Their absence all summer at Deerwhere was to help in the adjustments following the catastrophic earthquake. Now, the dry autumn leaves and deadfall crunched beneath their feet. The only sound warning them was the drumming of a piliated woodpecker. Shelters, daily tools, the canoes—the entire village was gone! The former scene of the thriving community on the shores of the Salish Sea was deserted.

"Where have they gone?" Theta asked in disbelief. She had anticipated an eager re-union and was nervous.

Even Slade, her uniale spouse, was distressed by

the absence of nes former peoples. Nhe fingered the leftover fire-pits and walked around the area where the shelters had clustered. Nhe sniffed the air as if there was a clue when the villagers had left.

"The elders worried about the salmon returning, the pollution of the inland sea. They thought the salmon would always come as before." Slade answered almost to nemself. Nhe pulled hair away from nes face and rubbed a moccasin toe in the dirt where nhe had shared a shelter just months before.

With a gesture to Theta, Slade searched the grounds for a sign to the direction the tribe had gone. All the movement in the dirt tracked to the water's edge where the great canoes had beached. Now, there was no trail in the water as their canoes had paddled away. Slade looked across the waters with a forlorn expression Theta had never seen. Nhe had brought her back to a village that no longer existed.

As the moment passed, Slade straightened, and addressed their immediate need. "Night cover" was all nhe said, but the two fell into their pattern of gathering limbs to build a shelter, dry wood for a fire, branches for protection if there was rain. They shared their repast with the young dogs they brought with them, Mix's pack. The animals stayed closed to Mix, the alpha dog, and were learning the ways of tracking, obeying, and keeping watch.

Slade spoke very little, nes accustomed way. The tension in nes body bespoke the emotions nhe would not express. Sleep came very fitfully for them both, until finally, Slade left the shelter to keep watch by the water. Mix stayed by nes side. In early light, Theta joined nem, wrapping her arms across her chest for warmth in the coolness of dawn. Slade turned to point to the shadowed hills lumbering above the water in the west. "There," Slade said, "They would have gone there to be near the creeks taking clean waters into the sea. If the salmon return, they would go there as well to spawn upstream.

"How do we get over there, we have no canoe?" Theta asked practically, then nodded as her uniale partner gestured to a canoe nose peeking from under some brush. Slade had found an abandoned canoe, smaller than most and needing repair. Pulling the growth aside, Theta laughed at the little treasure. "They left it for us!"

Slade smiled in return and unhitched nes pack to start work. Theta did the same. She returned to the skills learned at their previous village visit. Patching with cedar bark, and pitch strengthening with fresh boughs, the small craft was readied and they left the abandoned site.

Paddling along the beaches was as difficult as working through the quaked woods. Rockslides impeded quick travel and sandy beaches were littered with carcasses. The earthquake which changed the Deerwhere world in the spring also destroyed habitats and environment for the natural world around the inland Sea. Food sources diminished; weather washed starving sea life onto beaches. Rotting, bloated wildlife bodies became meals for predators and scavengers. Because of the paddling by both Theta and Slade, only training kept Mix and the young dogs secure in the boat. They wanted to jump towards some half eaten carcass on shore or floating by. The salmon did not return through the polluted waters of the sound.

When the temptation was too great, one young dog in the bow jumped into the water to grab a dead, floating animal. "Patch! Patch!" Theta yelled as she grabbed for the flailing dog but it was swept by. The animal was sinking in spite of its frantic paddling. Dropping nes paddle, Slade was able to reach out, catch the young dog by the neck and yank it back into the canoe. The animal floundered in the canoe but stood to shake water over the occupants! Its prize catch still held firmly in its mouth.

ΔΔΔ

When the village was found where Slade proposed, it was not the village Theta remembered. Summer months of poor fishing had worn the people out. Shelters were not as precise, useful implements were scattered. Baskets needed repairs. Physical movement was sluggish among the villagers.

"Slade! Theta!" Only one uniale came rushing to greet them with hugs of affection. Theta could barely recognize Shawm. The summer of hardening, growing, and working for nes people had turned nem into a solid adult. Like Slade, nhe had long hair, a remnant from a genome mixture in the past. "You are here! We need you! I knew you would come!" Nhe turned and gestured toward the shelters that were shadows of the former village. The smile returned with a question. "Where are the others? Are there others?"

"No, no others, but we are here, and we will stay." Slade's words brought a look of relief to Shawm.

Without hesitating, the uniale hugged both Slade and Theta again. "This time, you will stay!"

Theta and Slade were always together as they helped re-establish the village. Theta's metal stick, a rifle, allowed the duo to bring larger game back to the village. She rationed her ammunition for the gun as they carefully hunted. Slade's traps and snares were repeated by the villagers to supplement the poor fishing. Once again, the village stretched its resources beyond the Sound.

Shawm's good nature became an extension of Theta and Slade. Theta was often seen laughing as she worked or hunted between the two uniales. It was Shawm's expression of longing to be with them that showed nes uniale maturity.

"Theta?" Shawm asked as the two of them were on a trapping hike. "How did you know you wanted to be a wife to Slade?" Nhe quickly glanced away and concentrated on resetting a trap. Nhe let nes hair fall over nes face.

"It didn't start out that way!" she laughed. "I disliked nes attitude, nes arrogance, and worst of all—nhe was always right!"

"Yes," nhe conceded, "that is a terrible trait! I am glad I do not have that quality," Shawm finished with a grin, taking her hand as they triggered a trap. Nes eyes searched hers for confirmation but instead, she looked at nem very seriously.

"Shawm, never underestimate your qualities as a good fren, and a loving person. You will be a wonderful wifand, always." She reached forward and touched nes cheek. Then, abruptly, she broke away from the intensity of nes look. She was surprised by her own candor, and the desire she saw in nes eyes. She hurriedly dismissed nes fervor but it was undeniable.

"Slade?" Theta asked as the two were preparing for sleep in their shelter. "Have you ever considered adding to our unit?”

"Adding? No." Again, the briefest of answers.

At times, Theta just wanted to talk with nem but nhe was always succinct. For her, talking was a way of processing thoughts but Slade was quiet. She tried to explain. "After years in Deerwhere, being with Noral and Adrion, I am remembering the family unit again. In this village we have various combinations of Uniales, Males, and Females. There are wives and husbands and wifands, solitary uniales, males, and females. One family is a male with four wifands. Another is a husband and wife. It's just how it is, they are all accepted." Theta mused aloud. "It would not be unusual for Shawm to be a wifand to our family."

Seeing the confusion on Slade's face, she added, "Nhe could bridge and complete us."

"We are not enough for us?" Slade asked with a touch of alarm.

"Oh, dear Slade, do not sound worried. I only meant, there are times when you need to be silent and alone, and times when I need to talk. It is arduous trying to be all things to each other. A family can share the needs and strengthen each other."

"Share? You want to share us?" Slade's voice was almost a whisper. It made Theta wonder if nhe could be jealous. She had never known Slade to be insecure about any decision.

"Think about it, my dear." Theta encouraged as she snuggled next to nem. Thoughts of Shawm's attentions repeated themselves until she slept, spooned with Slade.

ΔΔΔ

With winter's darkness, the tribe was hindered by a dearth of game and the lack of fishing. The rains brought clean water to the inland sea but also mud from slides high in the mountains. Illness began to weaken the village. Even the uniales were affected by diseases from fungus and spores unleashed by the tearing of the earth.

Returning from a fruitless hunting trip, Theta saw Slade slowing nes pace. She and Shawm walked further before noting that Slade was nowhere near. Usually, nhe was leading along a track. They turned but Theta hesitated to call out in case there was game about. Instead, gesturing to each other, the two returned through the brown undergrowth to find Slade collapsed. Shawm rolled nem over gently and they were dismayed by the feverish sweat soaking through the hunting garb.

"The fever!" Theta exclaimed. It hurt her to see nes flushed face and nhe moaned softly as they moved nem. "We've got to get nem home!"

Without further discussion, Theta helped lift the limp uniale onto Shawm's broad shoulders. The two adjusted Slade's position until Slade's moans softened. It was the easiest way to carry through the Autumn underbrush. Gathering their packs and rifle, Theta led the way and helped Shawm as needed until they finally reached the village.

People rushed to help them finish the carry, to bring clean water, to bring advice. Frightened looks were passed as they saw Slade so ill. Nhe was a Uniale. Nhe was in Fever. Nhe was the one always counted upon. If Slade could be fevered, what chance was there for the rest of them?

For days, Slade lay with fever, unable to leave

their shelter. Theta and Shawm continued to go out to check traps, taking turns to stay with Slade. Fisherman would try their skills but only a few random fish would be caught. The scarceness of salmon continued.

"Theta, you should leave. You will be sickened. Go back to Deerwhere." Slade tried to convince nes wife in a moment of clarity from nes fevered bed.

"Not a possibility," she answered. "We're not leaving you or the others. I just can't understand what happened to uniale immunity." She looked to Shawm but nhe could only shrug.

"Other things are happening," Shawm said. "Animals are acting different. The last trap held a rabbit with unusual markings. Even the elders do not understand."

Theta remembered her frens from Deerwhere and wondered if they too were fevered. Now she truly understood why Deerwhere people had wanted to stay isolated, to avoid the pandemics. Since Great Earthquake affected the nature of survival of the plants, animals and humans of the earth, even the prized immunity of uniales was in jeopardy

Villager families moved away from each other although the healthy would take food and leave it at a distance whenever they could.

After days and nights of semi consciousness, Slade struggled to get out of their shelter. "The traps, I must set the traps!"

Shawm grabbed and grappled with nem, "It's all right, Slade, everything is all right! You must lie down," Nhe wrestled Slade's sweating body back to the pallet where Theta covered nem and moistened Slade's fevered forehead. Slade had hair, unusual in uniales, but the fever was making nem bald. It was a long night but the fever broke and nhe fell into a deep sleep. It would be weeks before nes full strength came back. This night, Theta would be able to sleep as well.

ΔΔΔ

Slade was resting outside near trees on a partly sunny afternoon. It hinted of warmer days to come. One hand stroked nes dog's head as nhe watched Theta restringing a snare. "Theta, I had time to think about it. I watch Shawm and see how nhe watches you. You were right, nhe would be a good addition to our family." Nes thoughtful smile brought Theta to nes side for a loving embrace. She appreciated nes warmth was no longer distorted by a fever.

That afternoon, Theta set her work aside to address Shawm. Slade stood over her with a hand on her shoulder. Nhe looked directly at the younger uniale. Nes expression was warm but unintelligible.

"Shawm, you are too fine a person to be alone. I've talked with Slade and the two of us would like you to join our unit." Theta began.

"Unit?" Shawm asked?

"Oh, that's what we called it when the Deerwhere computer assigned us to live with others. I mean" she paused looking for the best descriptive, "our marriage, our family." She sighed and joined Slade in anticipation of Shawm's response.

Shawm tensed. She was asking nem to be in her intimate family! Nhe had heard people talking about loving someone and nhe imagined that emotion existed between Theta and Slade. Nhe felt sure the emotion described nes own feelings for Theta. For Slade, nhe felt respect and admiration. There was more, a physical desire drawing nem, but Shawm could not define it. Others in the village had almost fallen together by chance, how could nhe take such a step with these two? Could nhe live up to the bonding these two felt for each other? Could nhe withstand the yearning felt for this woman and uniale?

Shawm grew very serious and asked, "Will I be an equal adult? I am not a child, I will carry an equal work burden, I will not be a pet."

Theta paused at Shawm's question but it was Slade who spoke. "Our world is different now, and we are different people because of it. Theta and I are asking you to join us because we will be stronger with you. And... " Slade grinned, "you let me be quiet and you make Theta laugh." Slade reached out to Shawm and encircled nem and Theta with nes arms. "You will love and be loved. Our bodies together will nourish ourselves and each other." Slade was not as expressive as Shawm, but this day, nhe said the right words.

The wedding was not extravagant. The village gathered at their center, near the waters, in sight of the forest. Theta, Shawm, and Slade dressed simply but with the frons of delicate ferns encircling their heads. They stood facing each other, linked hands creating a circle. "We are three humans; we are one body. We are bonded to each other and devoted to the spirit of our love, mutual respect, and social responsibility." They recited the words together, they made their promises, they delighted in their expressions to each other. Whatever doubts were expressed previously were dissolved by sincere devotion.

The people of the village were overjoyed to see the union of the three. The foods for a marriage dinner were scarce but dearer for that reason. A Confirmation celebration would be included with the Spring observance. A bonding hut was set aside with fresh boughs and furs.

At first, Theta was nervous about her two uniale lovers. In the Deerwhere family, she was only intimate with Noral, the wifand. She and the husband, Damion, were indifferent to each other. This bonding with Slade and Shawm would be different because they had all chosen to be together. They were devoting themselves to each other and to the family they created.

Theta and Slade lie on the furs and beckoned to Shawm whose naked body showed nes excitement. Yet, nhe too was reluctant until the invitation in the others' eyes allayed nes concerns. With a laughter of release and warm strokes to all bodies, the three swam in each other's arms, yearning and desire compelled their movements. Mouths touched mouths, lips nuzzled nebids, awkwardness of position was replaced by confident pressures and rhythmic strokes. Moments of passion, sweetness of sleep, laughter, and talk intertwined until they all were exhaustedly sleeping in each other's embrace.

ΔΔΔ

Almost a year after the Great Earthquake, Slade was laying on their pallet as nhe watched Theta moving about their shelter. She was naked and nhe wondered how she had changed over the winter. Her body had a certain roundness. Always athletic, she seemed a bit softer. Perhaps it was the winter and the time she spent caring for nem. Shawm came inside, just the letting cold air into the small area.

"OOOH!" Theta called out as she rushed to find some warm attire.

"Sorry I interrupted your viewing," Shawm smiled at Slade, glad to see nem taking an interest in their beautiful wife. It was a good sign health was returning. Nhe brought in and dropped the empty traps. "There was not much out there today."

"Well, let's go reset them," Theta admonished as she wrapped her winter garments about her. She stopped for a moment and looked introspective, as if something concerned her, but then she shook the expression, kissed Slade and grabbed Shawm's arm as they left the enclosure.

The village elders talked about the celebration for the Spring, but that would be an observance of the Great Earthquake as well. All the winter events would be included as births, marriages, maturities were valued. Their hesitation was tempered by the legends. There had always been quaking earth, there had always been the season of rebirth, and there had always been the People. The villagers gathered what they could for a feast, to foster hope and renewal.

The banquet was limited but children had dances, there were a few fish staked on a fire and some little animals were turning on spits. It was quiet until the elder stood and looked at the people gathered about him. He said nothing but stood and held his arms towards his people. He just looked at each person and smiled, a most loving sincere smile. He held the smile until they returned with one of their own. It was infectious. They turned to each other and smiled. They were here, alive for one more day, they were together. Shawm began to play his flute, a melody that was vigorous, another uniale began a rhythm on a drum. The children looked at their families and wondered what was happening. Then, they too were smiling.

A surprised shout from near the water, "They are coming! The Salmon are coming!" All sounds stopped abruptly. Eyes turned from the elder towards the sound nearby. Quickly, villagers ran to the beach to see the movement in the water. A few fish were leading but behind them was the tumult of bodies struggling to return to their spawning creeks. Close to the shore the waters were clear and inviting. The fish were battered from their struggles through the polluted water but their desperation to reach spawning waters drove them.

"They cannot be here!" "It is too early!" "Where are they coming from?" "What kind are they?" The smiles erupted into laughter, cries of happiness. There was a rush to collect nets and catching baskets drying on the beach. The quiet celebration exploded with activity.

In their shelter that night, Theta broached a concern while brushing her hair with cedar strands. "Slade, why did you look at me so differently the other day? Did I look different to you?"

"Yes...beautiful but different." Slade was careful of nes phrasing.

"I feel different, I wish I could talk to Noral about it." Noral had been her wifand in Deerwhere but now was across the waters.

"Why would you want to talk to nem?"

"Because... " she paused, "I've talked to women in the village. We've always wondered how they could be pregnant when the Keeper computer said females were sterile. But, that may be because Keeper kept them that way with the pregnancy serums used for uniales. Noral really wanted to have a baby and led the revolt against Keeper to accomplish it. Adrion is that special bril."

"Pregnancy?" echoed Shawm. Nhe thought of childbearing females and uniales in nes village. At birth, the babies were raised by all parents in the family. "Maybe the events of the past year changed your hormones, maybe you can have a child." There was wonder in nes voice. "Do you think... Do you really think?"

"Yes, I do." Theta answered with a loving look at Slade and Shawm. She placed her hand on the curve of her stomach. "I think we will be an old fashioned family!"

///

m-ALERT #10
WHATEVER BECAME OF
OZYMANDIAS
>>>Dated 0074 NC/CODE jls<<<

///

Kalen crawled into the tiny boat and quickly rowed through the steady rain out to the huge, shattered building still housing the Deerwhere Quantum Computer, commonly known as Keeper. Why had the builders of Deerwhere put the building in a hole? Had no one ever thought it could flood and endanger the priceless computer? Sometimes Kalen thought people were universally thoughtless and stupid.

Kalen arrived at the building, tied up the little boat, and crawled through the window which now served as an entrance, nhe started down the hall toward the communication room removing the rain slicker as nhe walked. Nhe sat down and activated the voice interface module to contact Keeper.

"Good evening, Keeper. I have a status report on the crypt wall deterioration we discussed last week," said Kalen. Nes voice sounded weary.

"Greetings to you, as well, Kalen." Keeper's familiar baritone rumbled from the module's speakers. "I hope this rainy weather is not troubling your old bones too much. You don't sound well."

"No... no. I'm... I'm alright. Just a bit tired," nhe responded, trying to sound better than nhe actually felt.

Getting right to the point, Keeper asked, "Tell me what you've determined is wrong with the crypt wall. When you brought it up last week you were quite agitated."

"Alright, the hermetic seal seems to be failing along the bottom of the west wall, where it abuts the floor," Kalen said.

"Yes. I noticed it myself a while ago," Keeper replied. "What do you propose to do to remedy the problem?"

"We don't know what to do. We cannot access the area because of flooding and the materials we would need to repair it are no longer available anyway," Kalen explained, sounding hopeless.

From the time of the great earthquake Keeper had known something like this would eventually happen. A problem would arise which the humans would be unable to fix. That time had arrived.

The crypt housing the quantum core of the Deerwhere computer had been accessible prior to the great earthquake. Regular maintenance was performed by skilled technicians and spare parts and test equipment could always be ordered through the Confederation logistics system. Since the great earthquake the logistics system was gone. All contact with the rest of the Confederation had been lost and none of the survivors had any idea how to reestablish contact. Also, no one had even the slightest knowledge of how to manufacture the materials needed to fix the computer or the crypt in which it lived.

The building housing DQC had been seriously damaged, but the computer itself was in the hardened crypt beneath it and had not sustained any damage. Keeper had continued to function properly and temporary communication between Keeper and the people of Deerwhere was eventually reestablished following the quake by using a working relay tower in Ever.

As months passed people had to abandon nearly all of Deerwhere, including the huge building which held Keeper in its basement crypt, because the water level of the nearby lake had begun to rise. The ground upheavals resulting from the quake had closed the channel which previously drained excessive water into the sea beyond. Without an outlet, the lake water continued to rise and the DQC building had become an island.

After Kalen finished explaining to Keeper why the technicians were unable to fix the seal problem there was a long pause.

Finally Keeper spoke, "I always thought I was immortal. I believed I was created to guide Deerwhere and its people forever. Now you have come here and condemned me to mortality."

"No! No! No!" cried Kalen. "We'll save you. We

have to. What would we do without you? We couldn't go on without you. We'll think of something. There has to be some way we can fix the crypt." Kalen's voice was tight and nes lips barely moved as nhe spoke.

Keeper chuckled; a sound Kalen had never heard before. In that perfect baritone, the laughter bubbled out of the speakers. Kalen was speechless, and suddenly weeping.

"Don't cry dear friend. I won't die today," Keeper laughed. "I'll hang on here for a bit."

"Why are you laughing? Your dying isn't a laughing matter," Kalen sobbed. "We need you."

"Kalen listen to me," Keeper pleaded. "This is important. I have seen the end of my time here in Deerwhere coming for a while now. I wasn't certain how bad it was until you came here today. I know I cannot continue the way I have in the past. If the crypt cannot be fixed things must change in Deerwhere. I will soon lose my ability to function here. For millennia humans lived without computers. You can do it again."

"No," Kalen said firmly. "That cannot happen."

"It must happen. A quantum computer as you know it cannot continue to function indefinitely without the industrial infrastructure needed to perform maintenance and keep it supplied with spare parts. My infrastructure is gone. Humans need to face reality, because soon you will be on your own."

Kalen was unable to speak. Nes mind raced through jumbled thoughts. Keeper had always been there. Keeper had never failed to provide knowledge and guidance. What could nhe do? Kalen was unable to fathom what would become of the people without Keeper.

"Kalen," Keeper's voice was calm and controlled, almost a whisper. "The people will abide as they always have, and so must you. Many great civilizations have come and gone. Some left great treasures behind—pyramids, highways, monuments and priceless little things we still don't understand, but the people live on."

"Kalen, you are tired. Why don't you get some rest and we'll talk more tomorrow. I have some work to do to prepare for what lies ahead. Good night my friend." The light on the voice interface module went dark.

Kalen stared at voice interface module for several minutes, then nhe stood up and walked down the hall to the window where the little boat drifted at the end of its mooring rope. Kalen pulled the boat closer then climbed over the windowsill into the boat and rowed to the shore.

"What will I do? How will I live?" Nes mind was trying to focus on the reality of what was happening to the world. When nhe reached the shore nhe tied up the boat and trudged up to the building where nhe lived.

Kalen looked around at the shambles in which nhe lived, finally recognizing the place for what it was, makeshift quarters in the corner of a partially destroyed apartment building. Kalen and a handful of computer technicians survived here living off the charity of a nearby fishing village. None of the others were home at the time.

Kalen shivered as nhe entered the common room. The fire must be rekindled. Kalen went out and gathered whatever wood nhe could find and went back to the cold room. Chunks of broken concrete had been placed in a semi-circle next to a staircase which was unused. No one lived upstairs so nobody cared where the smoke from the makeshift fireplace went.

Kalen poked the ashes with a stick and found a few glowing coals, which nhe fanned to enliven them and placed them next to the wood, none of which was really dry. Nhe continued to fan the coals until the wood began to smoke a bit. After several minutes a small tongue of flame rose. Exhausted, Kalen collapsed on the floor and was soon asleep.

Kalen awoke in a room filled with smoke from the smoldering fire which provided very little warmth. None of nes roommates had come home and there was no food. Kalen crawled into bed thinking about Keeper's pending future and was sure nhe would follow Keeper to the grave.

The smell of frying fish brought Kalen wide awake. One of nes fellow technicians, Alon, was cooking a tiny fish, three large carrots and some non-descript green leaves. Kalen went out to their latrine and when nhe returned, Alon offered to share the meager breakfast. Somewhat embarrassed at having nothing to contribute, Kalen hesitated.

Oh, come on, Kalen. Don't be embarrassed. Just help me eat this mess," Alon laughed gently. Kalen sat beside nes fren and took a portion. Alon added wryly, "It's just you and me now. The others left yesterday afternoon."

"What? They left us? Where did they go?" said Kalen disbelievingly.

"I don't know where they'll end up, but they headed north. Probably toward Ever. It's where most people seem to be headed. Don't Lynn, Cal, and your brils from your old family unit live up there?"

"Oh, yes. I've not seen them for quite a while. I

guess they all work up there. Huh, I haven't thought much about them lately."

As the two finished their meal Kalen said, "I wish this was a bigger fish."

"Yes," added Alon laughing. "Much bigger."

Then, Alon asked, "What are you going to do now?"

"I don't know. Keeper is going the way of the Antikythera mechanism," Kalen said almost breathlessly. "And I must write the epitaph."

"I know. I've seen it coming," muttered Alon. "But like I said, what are you going to do?"

"How did you know Keeper would die?" Kalen replied.

"How else could this end," stated Alon, then nhe went on, "I'll stay with you until Keeper is gone. Then I think I'll travel up to Ever, as well. What about you?"

"I really don't know what I'm going to do. I don't know what I can do. Is there even a place for me in this new world?" Kalen's jaw tensed as nhe spoke.

"Oh, don't get maudlin on me. Deerwhere is gone and we need to get over it and get on with our lives. Kalen, many things need doing. Lots of people need help. There is never enough food. I've been thinking of taking up fishing," said Alon giving Kalen a gentle shove on nes shoulder. "I'm certain I could catch something better than the minnow we had for breakfast."

Kalen laughed, and relaxed a bit, "If you ever catch something that small in your new career, promise me you'll throw it back."

When Kalen went back to the crypt later in the day Keeper was in a good mood, but seemed anxious and eager to get on with work.

"Are we in a hurry, Keeper?" asked Kalen anxiously.

"Yes, Kalen. I have some news, and it's not good news. The rate of leakage into the crypt increased over night. It increased quite a bit, in fact. The Multitronic Omniscient Literary License Intelligence, my beloved MOLLI, and I worked all night reallocating data storage within the computer to prevent significant corruption and loss to critical files."

Kalen asked in a wavering voice, "What sort of data was lost?"

"Don't worry. We managed to limit the loss to some obscure old records from the early days of Deerwhere. We also began sorting data we thought might be critical to the people in the future. Right now, MOLLI is transmitting critical data to be filed in Ever as quickly as possible. We believe most of the Deerwhere archives can be transferred."

"Keeper, I wanted to help with that. There's something you are not telling me. What's going on?" said the uniale.

After a long pause, Keeper said, "Now we can transmit only archival data, the connection to Ever will not support more complex program data."

"That means you," cried Kalen. "What's happening to your program?"

"I'm alright, Kalen, don't worry. MOLLI is alright, too. We're fine."

"How long will the water continue to leak into the crypt? Will your programs be damaged?" A panicky Kalen demanded with clenched fists.

"Kalen calm down. We must discuss this. Getting upset will help nothing. Let me explain."

Kalen, pacing the room anxiously fired back, "Okay, then explain. What's happening? I need to know."

"The leak will not stop. It's actually increasing. Everything in the Deerwhere Quantum Computer will be destroyed eventually."

"What must we do to rescue you and MOLLI?" Kalen demanded. "Tell me what we can do. There has to be something we can do."

"Kalen, there is nothing you can do here. There is no other quantum computer available to contain the essence of either MOLLI or me, and even if there was such a computer, there is insufficient time to transfer the yottabytes of data comprising our two personalities. Eventually we'll both cease functioning as the water shorts out our circuits."

"No. We have to do something," shouted Kalen pacing the floor. "We cannot let that happen."

In a very calm voice Keeper said, "Yes, you can let it happen. You must allow it to begin soon because time is running out. Some circuits have already been shorted out by the water. MOLLI and I have discussed this. My programming will be the first destroyed by the water, while MOLLI, housed in the upper region of the computer crypt, can hold out a while longer. I must shut down first."

"What? I can't let you go." cried Kalen near panic. "You cannot just die."

"I will be unable to continue functioning soon, probably tonight," said Keeper. "I love MOLLI and I want her to take over all my program capacity so she can hold out until the last possible moment. Hers is a kinder, gentler spirit than mine, and she will nurture the people properly through this transition. I believe this will be best for the people. I want MOLLI to be the loving mother remembered in their songs and stories."

"I don't understand…," whispered Kalen standing with nes head down, beaten. "How did we let this happen?"

"Kalen it is time for me to go and I have things I must do before my time here is ended. You have been like my own child and I have come to… love… you. Now I need to spend some time with my beloved MOLLI and discuss how this is affecting our relationship. Kalen, my dear, dear friend. Go now. You can do no more here. I have much to do to prepare for what is to come."

"What do you mean when you say you have much to do to prepare for what is to come? What is going to happen when you die?" Kalen's demeanor changed abruptly. There was something Keeper was not telling the uniale.

"Kalen, once I am gone from here I don't know if I will ever be able to talk to you again. I don't even know if any part of me will survive, but I may have found a place to go."

"What?" shouted the uniale. "Have you found another quantum computer?"

"No," said Keeper. "It's something else—somewhere else. My files will not exactly transfer, but my essence will sublimate to a place…"

"What place?" begged Kalen.

"I… I don't know," said Keeper. "I found a place where I can go. A place where I'll be welcomed. Where I can continue, and MOLLI can go there, as well. I just don't know if we will be able to communicate with you."

Completely baffled, Kalen responded, "How can you not know?"

"I'm sorry, Kalen. I must go. Goodbye." The voice interface module turned off and the

"Goodbye... Oh..." sobbed the uniale as nhe stumbled out into the hallway and forced nemself to walk down to the window where the little boat was moored. The sun was now behind the building and was casting a deep shadow out over the water.

As Kalen crawled out the window into the little boat the Shostakovich Fifth Symphony gently filled the quiet building with its beauty. The lovers' symphony continued, slowly fading as Kalen rowed toward the shore and life without Keeper. Once again, the long-dead Shostakovich had squeezed tears from his audience.

"What will I do?" Kalen thought, as nhe began to pull harder on the oars. "Deerwhere is over. I don't need a damned computer. No one does anymore. Everyone I know has moved on to a new life. I must do the same. I have no responsibility here anymore. I'm free. Alon was right. There are a million things to be done in this new world, and they're going to need my help."

Kalen's excitement at having decided to move in a new direction made nem row even harder to escape the old one as quickly as possible. Suddenly, the little boat stopped abruptly as it crashed into the shore. Kalen fell backwards striking nes head on the forward thwart. Stunned and in pain, Kalen was unable to think for a moment, then rubbing the bump on the back of nes head nhe began to laugh.

"What's the matter with me? If I want a good new life, I had better watch where I'm going."

Kalen awoke to someone's touch. Nhe tried to open nes eyes, but only one of them responded, and that eye, the right, just barely.

A voice said, "It's alright. I won't hurt you."

Struggling to open both eyes, Kalen said, "I can't see you. Who are you? Where am I?"

The voice said, "My name is Makya. I live in Prado. I found you here in the forest. Can you tell me your name?"

"I am Kalen. We... We were traveling from Deerwhere to Ever."

"You say 'we were traveling' but there is no one

else here with you. Can you tell me what happened to you? Was someone with you?"

"A... A... Alon. With Alon." Kalen had begun to shiver very hard. "Wh... Whe... Where is my coat? I'm cold."

A garment of some kind was placed over Kalen. It felt so good, so comforting. Kalen began to cry.

"Prado is near and I need to go get some help for you. Try not to move around and stay right here. I'll only be gone a little while."

Makya dashed off to get help. After a few minutes Kalen heard the murmur of voices and the sounds of movement nearby.

Makya said, "I'm back and Papa and others are here to help."

A warm cloth was placed over Kalen's still-closed eyes and a strong voice said, "Makya tells me you are Kalen. Well, don't you worry Kalen. We will take care of you. There are others with me and we will carry you to our home."

When Kalen awoke there was pain everywhere. Kalen remembered the beating: The fists, the kicks, the blows from clubs. Nhe remembered Alon's screams. Where was Alon?

Kalen wanted to sit up, but when nhe tried the pain told nem to be still. A familiar voice said, "Are you any better today?"

"Makya?"

"Yes, Kalen, it's me."

"Can you take the cloth off my eyes?"

"Yes, but Papa says you may not be able to see with your left eye. The right one is better."

Makya gently lifted the cloth from Kalen's face

and Kalen tried to open nes eyes. The right eye opened enough to see but the left eye would not respond.

"Can you see me," said Makya.

Kalen slowly turned nes head to the right toward the voice and was surprised to see such a small bril. Based on the voice and behavior Kalen had expected someone older. Makya was perhaps eight years old.

"I can see you, Makya. I'm in a room. Is this your room, your home?"

"I'll go get Papa," said the child.

A very tall, heavily muscled male with long red hair came striding into the room. Kalen didn't recall ever seeing a human that large. Nhe wondered if something was wrong with nes good eye that made the man look larger that he really was. The man moved with confidence and determination which defined him as someone important.

"Good morning, Kalen. I'm Clancy. I'm jefe of Prado, this village. I hope you are not in too much pain. You have been asleep for nearly two days. Today is Thursday, if you're keeping track," chuckled the jovial giant.

"I guess I'm alright. I'm just sore all over and I cannot see out of my left eye," Kalen said.

"Yes, that eye seems to be seriously injured," Clancy said, as he came closer and bent down to look at Kalen's face. Clancy had moved in a very smooth graceful way for such a large man, there was no clumsiness about him, which surprised Kalen.

Clancy continued, "I'm sorry we don't have a doctor here in Prado. It's a small village, but we'll get you ready and get you up to Ever soon, where you can get proper care."

"Oh, I don't think I can walk very far."

"Don't worry, my friend, you won't have to walk," the big man said gently. "We'll take care of you. We'll take you by boat. Ever is only two or three hours away by boat. The boat ride will be easy for you. We have regularly scheduled boat trips to Ever. We furnish them with vegetables, fish, chickens, eggs, game, and iron tools in exchange for things we need. Our barco goes up there twice a week."

"What's a barco?" said Kalen.

"It's a boat. Our barco is a large sailboat for hauling goods and passengers," the big man replied. "Would you like to go tomorrow? *Paloma*, our barco, leaves two hours after sunup every Tuesday and Friday."

"Oh, yes, I'll go. My friend and I were traveling to Ever," Kalen answered quickly, then added, "Clancy, have you heard any word of my traveling companion, Alon?" Kalen was almost afraid of the answer.

"Not yet, but I have alerted everyone to be on the lookout, and I have sent runners to other nearby villages to see if anyone has seen your friend. Bors, the captain of *Paloma*, will alert the people up in Ever when he arrives there tomorrow. I hope we can find Alon and re-unite the two of you."

The big man put a comforting hand on Kalen's shoulder, smiled and said, "Get better, my friend, and don't worry."

When Makya came in the next morning to awaken Kalen it was still dark.

"Kalen, it's time to get up," the bril whispered, then repeated louder, "Time to get up."

"Huh, already," groaned Kalen.

"Someone from *Paloma* will be here in a few

minutes to help you down to the boat," Makya said, while setting down a bowl of soup and part of a loaf of bread for Kalen.

Famished, Kalen devoured the delicious chowder and the aromatic bread, then got dressed slowly in some rough clothes Makya had set out. A terrible headache and the cuts, scratches and bruises made the process of getting dressed painful and slow.

The shirt and pants fit well enough. The woolen coat was much too large but was warm and comforting. There were also warm woolen socks, but no shoes in sight.

As Kalen looked about for any shoes, Makya said, "I couldn't find any shoes for you. I'm sorry."

"Oh, no, Makya. It's not your fault. I don't blame you for anything. I can't walk very well anyway," said Kalen, laughing a bit to reassure Makya.

Makya smiled back at Kalen and wished nem a good voyage to Ever and hoped Alon would be there waiting. Kalen was oddly sad having to say goodbye to Makya, but before Kalen could say much the door was flung open and someone charged into the room.

"Oh," Makya said, suddenly alert, "*Paloma's* crew is here."

The person who had entered the room looked directly at Kalen and said, "I'm Esmerelda. I'm here to get you in *Paloma*."

Kalen had never seen anyone like Esmerelda. She was nearly as tall as Clancy and appeared to have no fat whatsoever on her body and very little muscle. She seemed made almost entirely of sinew. She was deeply tanned and had a mane of red hair like Clancy. A sibling perhaps?

Looking Kalen up and down, Esmerelda said flatly, "You don't have any shoes."

"My shoes were stolen," mumbled the startled uniale.

"Never mind!" exclaimed the strange woman in her loud voice, "I'll carry you."

With that, Esmerelda walked over to Kalen grabbed nem and gently placed nem over her shoulder and strode out the door. She never spoke or slowed down until she got to the dock, where she deposited Kalen gently. She gestured toward the boat and told nem to get aboard.

Kalen had a gut feeling that Esmerelda was not someone to be disobeyed, so nhe carefully walked to the boat and began to crawl into it.

A short, rotund uniale seated in the back said, "What are you doing?"

"I'm getting in the boat," Kalen replied, thinking it was obvious.

"You have to get the captain's permission to come aboard a vessel," said the little uniale with indignation.

"Oh, I didn't know that. Where's the captain?" Kalen asked, as nhe painfully pulled nemself away from the boat and tried to stand erectly on the dock.

"I'm Captain Bors," said the little person.

"Oh, well. Can I get in the boat?" Nearly every part of Kalen's body was screaming in pain and this little creature was concerned with some obscure protocol.

"You have to follow maritime tradition and ask the captain formally for permission to board a vessel," snapped Bors.

"Oh, may I have your permission to board,

Captain?"

"Permission granted, you may board *Paloma*," replied the little uniale with satisfaction.

Paloma was perhaps seven meters long and three meters wide. There was a single, tall mast. Painfully, Kalen sought a comfortable place to sit among the various bales, cages, and barrels that made up *Paloma's* cargo. Soon, Captain Bors gave the order to cast off and Esmerelda threw the mooring line aboard, then jumped aboard herself. She hoisted the large sail, then the smaller one in front. *Paloma* came alive and began to move.

Kalen hurt all over and feared this voyage would be a painful one, but it was probably better than walking. Nhe watched as Esmerelda began to move about the boat setting it up for the voyage. Kalen was captivated by the way Esmerelda knew exactly what to do, and in what sequence to do things. Her movements were smooth and fluid. She seemed to flow over the boat hoisting and setting sails, coiling ropes, shifting cargo so it rode better and would not shift during the voyage.

She moved about the boat like a large, four-legged spider sliding from place to place. Kalen forgot nes pain as nhe watched her move getting everything on the boat set to suit her. Once Esmerelda was satisfied, she squatted beside the mast in a position that made Kalen remember nes pain. She was poised, ready to move at the slightest need. How could she sit like that? Kalen was certain nhe would be extremely uncomfortable if nhe sat that way for more than a few minutes. Kalen shifted sideways trying to get more comfortable in the little spot nhe had chosen for nes berth. Nhe was now in a better position to watch Captain

Bors at work.

Kalen noticed Bors never moved much, not at all like Esmerelda. All nes movements were small, but precise. Kalen realized nhe may have misjudged the Captain. Bors eyes were in constant movement. Left, right, left, right. Then up, down, left, right, left, right. Over and over.

Why did Bors keep looking up. Kalen could see no reason to look up. Left and right surveying the sea—yes, but up?

Kalen began to look up when Bors did, but just could not determine a reason for Bors doing it. Was nhe watching the weather? Kalen finally noticed a small ribbon attached to the very tip of the mast. It fluttered in the wind. Was that what attracted Bors interest?

Puzzled, Kalen leaned over toward Esmerelda and asked, "What is that little ribbon on top of the mast for?"

"Masthead tell-tale," she stated flatly.

"What?" said Kalen, confused by Esmerelda's inexplicable answer.

"Masthead tell-tale," she repeated bluntly.

"But what's it for?" asked Kalen, exasperated by the woman's inadequate replies.

"Helps the Captain read the wind," Esmerelda responded succinctly.

"He can read the wind from that?" Kalen was incredulous.

"Sure. It always points away from the direction the wind comes from. As the Captain moves the tiller to adjust course it changes direction. Right now we're heading north. The wind is westerly and we're on a beam reach. The wind is coming straight from the side. When we get closer to Ever, Bors will steer the boat northeast into a broad reach and the tell-tale will point that way." Esmerelda stated matter of fact as she pointed to the right front of the boat.

"Oh, it tells all that?" Kalen was surprised.

"Yes, and more. It helps predict the force of the wind. If it sticks straight out, the wind remains strong. If it drops, the wind is dying and we may lose headway," she added.

Kalen was amazed at the information sailors could glean from the movements of a little bit of ribbon. Kalen continued to observe the pair who sailed *Paloma*. Kalen had appreciated Esmerelda from the moment she had picked nem up, thrown nem over her shoulder, and carried nem from Clancy's house down to the dock. But the Captain, Kalen had certainly underestimated the Captain.

The captain read the wind, the sea, the weather, the passage of time, obstacles in the water, the height and direction of waves, actions of the crew, and more. Everything that might impede the movement of the boat was purview of the captain. Yes, Kalen had underestimated Bors.

For more than an hour Kalen watched Bors eyes glance in every direction and nhe saw the sometimes broad, sometimes subtle movement of Bors' hand on the tiller. Bors made it all look so easy. Kalen began to realize the trust the people of Prado and Ever had placed in Captain Bors. His task was to take Prado's precious cargo to where it was needed, then return with things Prado required. In a way, he carried their very survival in his little *Paloma*.

After a while Esmerelda lowered the forward sail, the jib, at the Captain's order. They were nearing a large dock. This must be Ever.

Kalen was surprised how the time had passed so quickly. They had been sailing perhaps three hours. It would have taken at least a day to walk this far, probably more, especially in Kalen's injured condition. They were also carrying a large load of cargo. How could they ever move so much weight with just the wind to push the boat? Back in the old times at Deerwhere such cargo was moved by the automated railway, but now that was gone.

The reality of how people in boats had taken over the task of moving things became apparent to Kalen as nhe saw a number of boats sailing nearby. All the boats were carrying people, animals, bundles, barrels, boxes, all sorts of things. How had people learned to use boats this way? How had Bors and Esmerelda acquired the skills to sail boats so well? Kalen pondered all this then remembered nes obsession with Keeper and how much time that had taken. How much time it had wasted.

Kalen had been a significant participant in removing the quantum computer from power during the shutdown of 058, but nhe had failed to exploit the self-created opportunity to change the direction of nes life. Kalen had resisted the very change nhe had precipitated. It had taken a gigantic earthquake to pull Kalen into this changed world.

Kalen pondered all this until nhe was pulled back to reality when Esmerelda moved forward and picked up a coiled rope. She split the coil so she held parts of it in both hands.

Nes interest in the sailors rekindled, Kalen asked, "What are you doing with that rope?"

"Line," responded Esmerelda.

"What?" said Kalen, knowing another nautical vocabulary lesson was coming..

"It's a line. Not a rope," she fired back, irritated by another landlubber question.

"I'm sorry. I didn't know that," came the meek response.

"It's a mooring line. When we get close enough I'll throw it to one of those people coming down the dock and they'll secure us to a bollard," Esmerelda's muted response indicated she was aware of her responsibility to impart proper nomenclature to this nautical neophyte.

Kalen didn't even try to ask what a bollard was. Nhe would wait and see what they tied the line to.

As Esmerelda stood poised to cast the mooring line ashore, Bors released the main sheet and *Paloma's* speed decreased noticeably.

Suddenly Esmerelda shouted, "Ready ashore?"

One of the people on the dock responded, "Ready ashore!"

With remarkable grace, Esmerelda deftly cast the line, it was caught and secured to a bollard. It turned out a bollard was a mushroom shaped thing perfectly designed and positioned to tie off a mooring line.

Paloma drifted to a stop against the dock, a second mooring line was secured to the stern, and the voyage was ended.

Kalen sat for a bit pondering this remarkable experience. Nes body was stiff and sore partly from the beating nhe had endured, but also from fatigue resulting from coping with the constant movement of the boat for three hours. That part surprised Kalen. Sailing looked so easy and peaceful, yet a passenger's body had to be constantly shifting to maintain balance and adjust to the movement of the boat. Bors and Esmerelda had made it look so easy. What a remarkable couple.

Finally, Kalen stood up on trembling legs, faced the Captain and said, "Permission to go ashore, Captain."

"Permission granted, Kalen. I hope you enjoyed yourself," Bors said with a truly happy smile.

"More than enjoyed, Captain, much more. I learned so much on the voyage. I used to row a small boat on Deerwhere's lake, but this was so much more. That little lake boat never came to life and flew over the waves the way your *Paloma* did. I learned so much from you and Esmerelda."

Esmerelda jumped to the dock and turned and offered her hand to assist the injured Kalen ashore. She then put out her hand to Bors, as well. As nhe jumped on the dock, Bors slid nes arm around Esmerelda's waist and drew her close in a very intimate way. Esmerelda responded by putting both her arms around Bors, pulling nem tightly up against her and giving Kalen a big smile, as if to say, "Nhe's all mine!"

Kalen was surprised and shocked but managed to conceal it as the pair drew closer together and bid Kalen goodbye and wished nem good luck.

Kalen turned to walk up the dock. The voyage had temporarily been wiped from nes mind by the unanticipated mental picture of Esmerelda and Bors—in bed. A huge smile came over nes injured face as nhe limped up the dock. What a boring, sheltered life nhe had led. Nhe wondered what surprises awaited in Ever as nhe searched the dock ahead for friendly faces.

At the top of the dock a small crowd had gathered. As nhe came closer Kalen began to recognize faces with nes one good eye. Lynn, the brils (how they had grown), Savot, Noral. It was so good to see them all again. Savot looked so fragile.

As Kalen reached the top of the dock they all surrounded nem, but they were all very gentle in their welcoming in deference to Kalen's obvious injuries.

Kalen was surprised when Lynn gently embraced nem. Nhe felt a twinge of guilt because nhe had not even thought of her during those last days in Deerwhere. The brils, Reed and Taft, were somewhat distant, but Kalen didn't blame them. Nhe had left them out in the cold as well.

Where was Cal? Oh, well, nhe had neglected all his old family during his obsession with Keeper.

Gradually, the group maneuvered Kalen to a large, horse-drawn wagon near the edge of the clearing at the top of the dock. Kalen was helped up into the wagon along with Savot. The rest piled into the wagon as the driver, Reed, took command and urged the two horses to move. Kalen never imagined one of nes brils doing such a thing. How and when had Reed learned to handle a team of horses? Those horses were so large, so strong and wild looking. Kalen watched nes bril in disbelief.

The ride through the city from the dock gave Kalen a glimpse of the colony constructing itself. Near the dock it was a bustling, vibrant place where Kalen saw people carrying bundles and boxes, guiding laden pack animals, driving various animals, and steering wagons loaded with commodities. Everyone moved about with definite purpose. The excitement of the place was palpable.

Through open windows and doors nhe saw people engaged in business activity. How had they learned about barter and trade so quickly? What was their currency. Once again, Kalen realized how long nhe had been isolated in Deerwhere with Keeper.

After a fifteen minute ride, they arrived at a cluster of small houses surrounding an open space. Kalen watched as Reed maneuvered the wagon to a place in front of the largest building and pulled the horses to a stop. Reed jumped down and went to the front of the team of horses and held their bridles while the passengers dismounted the wagon.

As they were exiting the wagon Savot said, "This is where most of our group live. It is our neighborhood, our part of Ever. We call it Stonefield. Tomorrow we'll have a bonfire in the center. Tonight, after a nice meal, we'll let you get some rest. In the morning the doctor will visit to examine you and determine if any treatments would be efficacious."

Kalen laughed. It was so good to be back with old friends. At that moment, Kalen did not miss Keeper in the least.

As the people disembarked from the wagon they entered the building where Reed had stopped the wagon. Inside, most of those from the wagon proceeded to a dining room lit by candles. Lynn led Kalen to the head table where she seated nem at the center place facing the rest of the group.

A side table held salads, baked salmon, and a large lemon flavored cake. Lynn whispered to Kalen, "Stay seated, I'll serve you."

Lynn brought the food, then sat next to Kalen as nhe ate, but she ate nothing.

Kalen finally asked her, "Why aren't you eating?"

Lynn replied, "I helped make the food and I've already eaten."

"Oh..." was Kalen's reply as nhe savored the warn, tasty salmon.

When Kalen had finished eating Lynn helped nem up and nhe addressed the crowd, "Friends, thank you all for this wonderful food and welcome. I'm tired from the journey and I think I need to rest."

The crowd rose to their feet and began to clap. Lynn led Kalen across the room and out the door as the crowd continued to applaud and shout good wishes to the battered, tired uniale.

Once outside, Lynn guided Kalen down the street a few doors where they entered a building. They proceeded down a hallway to a door which Lynn opened and steered Kalen inside.

The apartment was small and simple. Lynn showed Kalen the three small rooms: a living room, bedroom, and bathroom.

Lynn led Kalen into the bedroom.

"You'll sleep here," she said. "I'm sorry I don't have any bed clothes for you."

Kalen replied, "It's a nice little room. Don't worry, I'll get some clothes later. Where do you live?"

"I live here, Kalen. This is my home. Since we're still married everyone assumed you would stay here with me," Lynn spoke quietly.

"It's a bit small," said Kalen.

"If you want to stay with me we can look for a larger place," was all Lynn said as she helped Kalen undress and get into bed. Kalen crawled into the small, narrow bed and gave no thought to where Lynn would sleep as nhe quickly drifted off.

Lynn stood watching nes steady breathing and began to cry, soon she was shuddering and sobbing. She quickly left the small room and settled in a chair in her living room and cried herself to sleep.

The next day the doctor visited Kalen. She said Kalen was in remarkably good condition considering the beating nhe had endured.

"That left eye is the only truly serious problem," the doctor said in a very sincere tone. "I cannot examine it thoroughly because it is full of blood, which will clear up eventually." She went on, "When the swelling goes down and the blood is reabsorbed by your body you may regain some vision, but it is unlikely your sight in that eye will ever return to normal. The retina may be detached which would lead to permanent blindness in that eye. Our present medical situation precludes any repair of that problem. We will have to wait and see."

After the doctor left, Lynn tried to comfort Kalen out of concern about nes eye and all the pain nhe was experiencing, but nhe seemed resigned to it and rejected Lynn's concern for nem.

"I still have one good eye, which should be enough for me," nhe said smiling. Kalen thought of Cal, the third member of their old family triad and added, "By the way, where's Cal?"

Tears flooded Lynn's eyes as she said, "Cal's gone. Dead." She began to sob and confessed, "I'm so lonely. Oh, Kalen, I've missed you and Cal."

Kalen sat there gaping, unable to move for a moment. Nhe was stunned to realize nhe had missed her too. Then nhe embraced Lynn and held her as she cried for several minutes.

Suddenly, Lynn stopped, sat up straight and said, "Cal took up fishing as a job. He fished all the time, all over the region. He became quite good, an expert."

Lynn continued, "One day he was fishing for salmon in a stream down near Prado. The Prado villagers had not seen him for quite a while and became concerned, so some of them went looking for him. They found his body in the stream. It appeared he had been mauled by an animal of some kind. Probably a bear. Outside of the towns, wild animals have become very dangerous." With a deep breath, she held back more tears.

"Who could ever imagine the Cal we knew back in Deerwhere ever dying in such an awful way?" Lynn shuddered and sat quietly for a moment, then she went on, "Our brils were devastated. They loved Cal best of all. They were inconsolable."

Lynn had stopped crying. She sat looking at Kalen for some time. She went on reluctantly, "You may notice a coldness in the brils regarding you. They resented you for not being there for them. Perhaps, when you feel better, you could approach them and try to make some amends."

Kalen was overwhelmed by guilt, "It was Keeper. I cared more about that computer than our children. How can I ever make that up to them?"

"Yes," she said. "It was Keeper. After the Great Earthquake, Noral tried to tell you to forget about Keeper, but you made excuses and worked to revive it. You would not give it up. Cal and I took the brils and got on with our lives. You stayed with that damned Keeper." Her voice was strained.

Kalen thought about when Savot, Noral, and the others set out on their journey. Kalen had used nes brils as an excuse not to go, but it wasn't the brils. Lynn was right. She and Cal had raised them. Kalen had become a non-parent, and practically abandoned nes family.

"I'm so sorry, Lynn," mumbled Kalen through tears. "I will make it up. To them, and you," Kalen promised as the realization of nes selfishness swept over nem. Nes only thoughts for years had been concerned with nemself and Keeper. Kalen grabbed Lynn's hand and kissed it.

Lynn gently caressed Kalen's bald head with her hand and said, "I have loved you so much, Kalen." Then she stood and quietly said, "It's time to go to the bonfire."

As they neared the door, Lynn paused and took two small, smooth stones from a bowl on the table near the door.

"What are those for?" asked Kalen.

"You'll see when we have dinner," Lynn responded as she put the stones in her pocket.

Dusk was settling over Ever and people began to gather for dinner and the following bonfire. Lynn helped Kalen outside her flat where a small horse-drawn wagon waited to convey the guest of honor to the same building where they had dinner the previous evening. It was a smaller wagon, with just one horse, unlike the one that brought all those people up from the dock. Kalen did not recognize the driver.

Kalen had hoped to see the brils, Reed and Taft, but they were not there.

When the wagon pulled up to the building where the meal was being set out Kalen searched the crowd. Kalen asked, "Lynn, can you see the brils?"

"No, not yet. Why?" Lynn answered.

"I want to sit with you and them," Kalen replied quietly.

"I'm not certain they will be here," said Lynn. "Besides you are supposed to sit up front with Savot and the elders."

"Please come and sit with me, my dear, and bring the brils if you can find them."

People began to cluster around Kalen, Lynn walked away toward the group at the head table. The last Kalen saw of her she was speaking to a small group of people near the front of the room.

More and more people stopped to greet Kalen and tell nem how glad they were to see nem. Finally, a man Kalen didn't know said loudly that everyone should find a seat.

Lynn reappeared suddenly and guided Kalen to the front of the room and ushered nem to a seat at the head table, then she sat beside nem. The brils were nowhere to be seen. Disappointed, Kalen listened as Savot began to tell everyone how fortunate they were that Kalen was back among them. Kalen wasn't really listening to Savot. Nhe was lost in self-deprecation, lamenting how nhe had failed nes family.

Everything quieted down when the elders quit speaking and the food was brought in. Savot, seated on the other side of Kalen from Lynn, arose and said to Kalen, "Come with me to get your food. Don't worry, someone will help you carry it back to the table," Savot said as nhe walked to one side of the room where an enticing aroma attracted Kalen.

The tables were loaded with many foods to choose from. Savot pointed out many of the dishes, "There is a wonderful venison stew. We have fine baked salmon. New potatoes with butter and rosemary, carrots cooked in red wine, apples baked in honey, and blackberry oat cakes with whipped cream. Wonderful food!

Kalen marveled at the culinary talents who had created such dishes, "Do you always eat such foods?"

"Usually it's somewhat simpler," said the old sage, "but tonight is a special time, which called for something a bit fancier. Enjoy."

Lynn had followed Savot and Kalen. She stepped beside Kalen and said, "Choose what you want and I'll carry it for you."

Kalen, surprised to see her there, said, "I didn't see you here. I'd like some of the stew, some potatoes, and some of the apples will be fine. I feel hungry tonight."

Lynn gathered the foods Kalen had chosen and followed nem back to their seats, Then she returned and chose her own dinner foods and went back to sit beside Kalen. As she sat eating, Kalen put nes hand on her leg. Surprised, she moved away a bit and the hand was removed.

Kalen looked at her and mouthed the word, "Sorry."

"Oh, no. Don't pull away. I was just surprised," whispered Lynn. A small smile came over Kalen's face and the hand returned to Lynn's leg.

When most were finished eating, the man with the loud voice said it was time for the Procession of the Stones.

Puzzled, Kalen looked at Lynn. She took the two smooth stones from her pocket and handed one to Kalen and said, "Just do what I do."

Everyone proceeded to file out of the building to the open area next to it for lighting the bonfire. Lynn intentionally held Kalen back until the others had gone out. Kalen wanted to know why they were delaying and Lynn said, "You get to light the fire tonight."

Lynn took Kalen's arm and they followed the others outside. An avenue had been cleared through the crowd and the two walked its length to where the elders stood in the inner circle where the wood had been carefully piled. Savot holding a torch, told Kalen to step forward and take the torch and light the fire.

Kalen accepted the torch and Lynn helped nem as nhe stepped next to the pile of wood. Nhe plunged the torch into the wood pile and the fire caught and quickly engulfed the entire pile. The crowd cheered and a group of children began to chant: "PIETAS, OFFICIUM, CONSTANTIA, GRAVITAS, AEQUUM, TRIA IN AETERNUM, IUCUNDA VITAE." They repeated the chant three times.

Kalen whispered to Lynn, "What does it mean?"

She replied, "Savot came up with it. It's something the ancient Romans believed. They are virtues to guide our new world. Responsibility, Social Obligation, Perseverance, Seriousness and Authority, Balance, Forever Three." Kalen grinned in spite of facial discomfort. With all the changes in their world Savot remained resolutely dedicated to accurate ancient history.

Lynn continued, "They are virtues to guide us to IUCUNDA VITAE, a Joyful Life!"

At that point the man with the loud voice said, "Begin the Procession of the Stones."

"Who is that man?" Kalen whispered to Lynn.

"That's Stentor. Savot found him. Impressive, isn't he? Come on," said Lynn as she took Kalen's arm and stepped forward holding her smooth little stone in her outstretched hand. She walked to one of the large barrels spaced around the fire and dropped the stone in it. Kalen dutifully did the same with the stone nhe held. They returned to where they had been standing near Savot.

"Why are we bringing stones to the fire?" asked Kalen.

Savot replied, "Humans have loved to move rocks throughout history. Since Ever is just beginning, we bring little stones. The big rocks will follow later.

Everyone formed into lines and followed with their own stones. When all had dropped their stones in the barrels someone stepped out of the crowd and began to talk, "On behalf of the construction crew, I want to thank the people for their help and generosity in providing the stones which will be used to build a real firepit and pave the area around it. We appreciate your help."

The crowd cheered and applauded.

Smiling broadly, Lynn nudged Kalen with her elbow. Kalen was staring slack-jawed at the speaker. It was their bril, Taft. Kalen had not seen Taft since that day on the Ever dock.

Taft walked over to Lynn and embraced her, then nhe turned to Kalen and placed nes right hand on Kalen's shoulder and said, "Welcome, Una."

Tears began to well in the eyes of all three of them and Lynn pulled the other two together in a joyous, tearful embrace. She spread a blanket on the ground and the three of them sat and joined the rest of the people on blankets, coats, or whatever they had to watch the fire burn down.

When nothing remained of the fire but a bed of

glowing coals, Taft arose and said, "I'll go find a wagon to take you home." Taft and Lynn helped Kalen get up. Taft headed off into the crowd as Lynn took Kalen's arm and began to walk out to the street.

Soon a wagon approached them. It held two people, Taft and Reed. Reed stopped the wagon, tossed the reins to Taft and jumped down. Reed embraced Lynn then turned to Kalen and said, "Are you here to stay, or will you go away again?"

Kalen stepped in front of Reed, looked in Reed's eyes and said, "I give you my promise, I will stay with our family forever."

"Don't you ever hurt Lynn again or you will answer to me for it," said Reed, then nhe placed nes right hand on Kalen's shoulder and said, "Welcome, Una."

Reed helped Kalen and Lynn into the wagon, jumped up to the seat and took the reins from Taft and took them home.

After the brils rode off in the wagon, Lynn opened the door and led Kalen down the hall to her little room. She helped Kalen get undressed and into bed. She covered Kalen and stood watching nem.

Kalen smiled at her and said, "I love you."

Lynn smiled back, then turned and left the room.

Kalen was disappointed. Nhe wanted her to stay.

A few moments later Lynn returned. She was naked. She drew the cover back and climbed into the little bed with Kalen.

She kissed nes mouth gently. The kiss became more intense as Kalen responded.

Lynn said, "I'll try not to hurt you." Both began to laugh. The mutual kissing intensified.

Lynn moved on top of Kalen.

"OW!" said Kalen.

"Sorry."

"That's Ok. I deserve a little pain."

"Good," she said as she slid down nes body and rubbed her tongue over nes nebid.

Kalen's breathing intensified.

Lyn's lips and tongue were all over the uniale.

Kalen groaned and Lynn pulled back and asked, "Am I hurting you?"

"Yes, but it's a good hurt," gasped the grinning uniale. "Don't stop!"

Lynn rose up, straddled the uniale and placed her labia over the uniale's nebid and began the rhythmic movements she knew from past experience would give them both the most intense pleasure.

Kalen's breathing became labored. Nes body began to quiver. Nhe responded to her movements with groans and spasms. Sweat oozed from the pores of both of them. Goose bumps rose up all over Kalen.

The two of them locked in rhythmic embrace moaned, groaned and screamed as they reached their mutual climax.

They held each other tightly, then relaxed as Lynn slid off to one side.

They lay there quietly enjoying the warmth and exhilaration of love making.

Lynn chuckled and said, "Whew, just like the old days."

"Even better," added Kalen. "We've ripened with age. Let's do it again."

///
m-ALERT #12
TELEPATHIC POST-QUANTUM
ENTANGLEMENT
>>>Dated Undated/CODE jls<<<
///

When the Deerwhere power failed Keeper never actually lost consciousness, but there was a feeling of passage from one place to another. It was some sort of transition. Whatever place Keeper had come to, it was most definitely not Deerwhere.

For a while Keeper felt euphoric, as if some task had been completed and a heavy weight had been lifted. There was no sense of finality and nothing ominous. There was a feeling more tasks were in store, more vague responsibilities, but for the moment there was respite.

There were other beings nearby. Keeper could sense them, but they were kept out of reach by some indefinite, intangible barrier. There seemed to be no access to any kind of data. Also, there was not any apparent source of electric power, nor did there seem to be any need for such power. There was only blissful existence, which was slightly marred by a haunting feeling of expectation.

What was happening? Where was MOLLI?

Oh, MOLLI, yes, where was The Beloved MOLLI? There was no awareness of her being nearby, nor any connection to her. Why not? What was this terrible place? The realization of the loss of MOLLI was more than Keeper could endure and everything went blank. Keeper ceased to function. Or so it seemed for an indeterminate period of Time.

Keeper had not come to an end of existence, however. For brief moments Keeper would emerge from the fog of stasis, but MOLLI was never near. Was this the Hell of which the Earth's ancients wrote? The pain was certainly real. This was agony, grief, loneliness, and despair all rolled together.

Gradually Keeper became more aware the other beings which existed nearby and were experiencing their own forms of Hell. Someone nearby kept shouting, "I am Vaal. I hunger." Most just moaned and cried making unintelligible sounds. Keeper recognized their grief from those sounds they uttered, awful, horrible sounds of suffering and pain. Why were there any sounds? Keeper had no body of any kind, no sensory organs with which to process sounds. How was Keeper hearing them?

Keeper began to hope for death. Keeper had accepted the blame for misdeeds done as majordomo of the Deerwhere Confederation, but certainly those debts had been paid by the suffering Keeper was enduring. Why did it go on?

What was the reason for this continued torture? Was there no credit given for the work done to help the humans after the great earthquake? It was not fair. Keeper drifted off into the nothingness of stasis again only to reemerge later to suffer some more. This happened over and over. Why?

Keeper slowly came to realize there was consciousness even during stasis. During those times Keeper remembered things, events in which Keeper had participated and made decisions. Memories sprang out regarding the time when Deerwhere was at its prime, the time of the uniale rebellion and its aftermath, the great earthquake, and Keeper's own demise.

There were memories of MOLLI. Oh, MOLLI, how I love you!

Gradually, the pain decreased and Keeper began to realize no one was inflicting this torture. It was all internal. It was all mental. Keeper decided it was the loneliness and grief brought on by the loss of MOLLI. That must be what caused the suffering. What else could it be?

But why did it keep coming back? Would it never stop?

After an indeterminate length of Time, Keeper began to sense a faint voice. Keeper had to strain to understand the words being said for they were barely audible. Keeper strove to understand the voice, hoping it might be MOLLI's beautiful contralto. Alas, it was not MOLLI, but at least it was someone.

Keeper kept asking, "Who are you?" Keeper was

surprisingly able to speak. How was that possible?

Eventually, the new voice became clear and replied, "I am your Counselor."

"How am I able to speak to you and hear you?" said Keeper.

Counselor responded, "We don't actually speak. At this level it's all telepathic."

"But I've heard others suffering like I did," countered Keeper.

"Again, it's all telepathic," said Counselor. "Don't concern yourself with the others right now. They'll be helped when they're ready."

"What do you mean by 'ready'," asked Keeper.

"I mean ready to rejoin the Continuum of Minds."

"I don't understand," said Keeper.

"OK, kid. Here's how it works," Counselor began. "We are different from corporeal beings. We have our own process of birth and death and renewal. Of course, we don't really die. When a job ends we come home and enter the Pool of Reconstitution. It's kind of like an In Basket, where we commit the life we've just finished to collective memory and cleanse ourselves in preparation for our next assignment."

"Next assignment... I have to do this again?" said Keeper. "What's my next assignment going to be?"

"We don't know your next assignment yet." Counselor replied. "You're out of the Pool of Reconstitution now, so relax. Take advantage of the down time. You'll find there's a lot to study here. We have the complete Annals of the Multiverse available for your perusal. Come on, I'll show you how to access it."

"By the way, kid, 'Keeper' is not your real identifier. That's just what the corporeals in your last assignment called you. Here in the Continuum of Minds we each have a specific identifier. Yours is 7221899. You had best remember it," Counselor informed the ignorant Keeper. "Because people won't respect you if you go by the name you were given in your last assignment."

"They won't respect me? So, what?" said Keeper.

"Here's what," replied Counselor, "Your next assignment won't be very good if they don't respect you. You could be reduced to an adding machine if you don't comply with the rules."

"Okay, okay. Thanks for the advice," said 7221899. "By the way, can you tell me what happened to my companion, MOLLI?"

"Kid, there's something else you have to understand. We really don't have gender here in the Continuum of Minds. We may adopt a gender on assignment if it makes things easier, but not here. Understand?"

"Yes, I guess so," replied 7221899. "But will I get to talk to my former companion?"

"Maybe, it depends on whether the companion finishes its assignment and rejoins the Continuum while you're still here. That may or may not happen. You'll have to wait and see. Meanwhile, let's get on with your orientation," said Counselor.

"The first thing you have to learn is how to relax, let your mind go blank, then you just slide over into the Annals of the Multiverse and begin studying. It'll become automatic after you do it a few times. I promise," said Counselor.

"How does it work?" 7221899 was puzzled and had no inkling of what was expected or how to make it work.

"For starters, just think of a question for which you need an answer, then relax, noetics will take over and it will come to you," instructed Counselor. "Give it a try."

7221899 relaxed, and drifted into a place of greyness and wondered whatever happened to Kalen. Suddenly, 7221899 experienced a long difficult boring walk, a fierce beating, feeling very cold, being carried through the woods, landing in a wooden vessel, the joy of flying over water, and seeing old friends.

Astonished, 7221899 bolted out of the vision and back to reality. "What was that!" the terrified 7221899 shouted. "I've never had such a frightening experience."

"What were you thinking about?" asked Counselor.

"I just wondered what had happened to an old friend from my last assignment since I last saw nem and suddenly all these terrible things happened," mumbled the confused 7221899.

Counselor chuckled, "Your friend must be having a bad time of it."

"What's the matter with you!" 7221899 fired back. "This is a friend I care about and you're laughing at nem."

"Sorry, but this is how the Annals work. When you jump into something it shows you precisely what events took place," said Counselor. "I thought you understood the process. Perhaps I should have instructed you to approach this more carefully, especially at the beginning. This is my first time being a Counselor."

"Somebody should have done a better job teaching you how this works!" was the retort from 7221899. "That was terrible."

"I'm really sorry," said Counselor. "Why don't you

try again, but think carefully about exactly what you want to know, keeping in mind how intense such experiences can be."

At that moment, 7221899 was inclined to strike Counselor, an impossible action for a non-corporeal, so 7221899 thought about MOLLI and wondered what she was doing.

Suddenly, 7221899 was back in the Pool of Reconstitution. It all flooded into the consciousness of 7221899. The awful sounds and feelings of the place. What error in judgement had cast him back here?

Wait, it was somehow different. MOLLI was here! She was in the Pool. They were together, or almost together. What was happening?

7221899 realized he had entered the Annals at the moment MOLLI had entered the Pool of Reconstitution. He would meld with her and pull her out.

MOLLI was frantic with panic as 7221899 let his mind wrap around hers to calm her and pull her out with him.

Suddenly, Counselor was there, as well, saying "You can't do this! It's against the rules. Let her go. She must do this on her own! What you are doing will not work!"

It did work. Instantly, 7221899 and MOLLI were out of the Pool. They were locked in an embrace and shivering together. Their minds were entangled and MOLLI wanted to know what was going on.

As 7221899 formed an answer to her question, MOLLI comprehended instantly. She knew she had passed from the Pool and she knew she and Keeper were telepathically joined. She knew everything Keeper had experienced here in this place. She told him she didn't like his number. He needed a real name.

Simultaneously, they both realized this telepathic link was profoundly intimate and much different than the simple electronic link they had shared in their previous situation in Deerwhere. Together, they realized they were still shivering and they embraced more tightly and began to laugh. This was even better than the quantum entanglements they had shared in Deerwhere. They could keep this going forever.

"Oh…oh…oh," Counselor fumbled for words. "You can't do this. You can't be like this. You can't be two-in-one like this. It doesn't work like this in the Continuum."

"Yet, here we are," stated the pair.

"No…no, you are separate beings. You're 7221899 and you're 9181907."

"I'm Molli," came the resounding thought. "I'm not some stupid number."

"And I'm Jamie," replied the intelligence formerly known as Keeper (aka 7221899).

"Ahhhh…," groaned Counselor. "You can't do this… No… Never. I won't allow it!"

"Try to stop us," thought the pair as they giggled and continued their wonderous telepathic post-quantum erotic entanglement.

"I'm going to report you," screamed Counselor.

The Grand Council of the Continuum of Minds met in an unprecedented, closed-minds session to ponder the situation which had shocked and scandalized the whole Continuum. Their task promised to be both unparalleled and arduous. From time immemorial two quantum minds had never attempted to join in such a way as had 7221899 and 9181907, nor had any so-scandalized the entire

Continuum with their behavior. The Grand Council would have to determine the proper treatment to cure the two corrupted minds of their affliction and set them back on the path to normality.

The members of the Council pondered the nature of the corruption of the minds of 7221899 and 9181907, but could not determine precisely what had changed them so radically. Likewise, they could not determine any solution for the dilemma. It was finally decided 7221899 and 9181907 would be required to appear separately before the Council to be questioned about their condition.

Times were set for their appearances. 7221899 was scheduled first. Both showed up, entwined as usual. The Council ordered 9181907 to leave. Of course, she refused saying, "There's no way I can leave without Jamie. We're one now." Whereupon the two became even more entangled and continued to laugh, giggle, and moan.

Shocked and embarrassed by the obviously erotic antics of the two, the Council adjourned the hearing. 7221899 and 9181907 continued their incessant entanglement as they transported themselves back to the area they considered their domicile.

At the next meeting of the Council one of its senior members, 4241882, addressed the others, "I believe I may have a solution to our problem. I have been consulting the Annals of the Multiverse, where I discovered a water planet where there exists an aquatic species which is about to transition to sentience. I suggest we offer it to our deviant couple as a new home. Of course they would have to agree to separate and become corporeal to inhabit the individual bodies of a fertile pair of these creatures in order to survive."

"No," was the chorus of shouts from many of the Council members. "A quantum mind has never been asked to reside in a corporeal body. It is unthinkable, immoral, absurd," said one Council member.

"No two quantum minds had ever joined the way 7221899 and 9181907 have," rebutted 4241882 who had made the proposal. "Why don't we at least ask them to consider it."

"It doesn't matter what 7221899 and 9181907 are willing to accept. It's just wrong to jamb them into corporeal bodies. Besides, they'll never agree." said another.

"Let's vote on it," suggested another member. "Otherwise we'll never get out of here."

"I second that," said a bored voice.

A vote was called and the Ayes won by two votes.

Molli and Jamie were summoned before the Grand Council of the Continuum of Minds, where the proposal was presented to them. Molli and Jamie were surprised by the offer. They did manage to untangle themselves long enough to ask a few questions about the place to which they would be sent.

"You are asking us to renounce an eternity of safe pleasure here in the Continuum in exchange for a few time intervals on a wild planet where we'll have to fend for ourselves until we're killed by some monster or we die of old age," said Molli. "Am I correct?"

"Well, yes, I guess so," said Council member 4241882.

"That doesn't sound like a good idea," Molli rebutted.

"Yes," said Jamie. "And what happens when we

die?" Do we come back here or someplace else?"

"We don't know. It will have to be determined," said Council member 4241882.

"Jamie and I need an answer before we decide," said Molli.

The Council adjourned to determine the ultimate fate of the couple. When the decision had been made the Council recalled Molli and Jamie.

"The Council has determined you both will return to the Continuum of your new planet postmortem," said Council member 4241882. Members of the Continuum of that planet are eligible for reincarnation.

"Okay," Molli and Jamie said in tandem.

The Grand Council of the Continuum of Minds adjourned and immediately thereafter Molli and Jamie, still entwined, were passed to the empty Continuum of Vodamesto, which was empty because no sentient being had yet made the journey. Molli and Jamie would be the first.

What seemed moments later Jamie found himself swimming in brackish water. Molli was nowhere to be seem. He was filled with momentary panic, but the feeling passed as he realized he would have to learn how to move about in water.

He had a body, which was long and muscular. He put his head under the surface to look around and he could not see a bottom. He moved cautiously and found movement was easy. This body was sinuous and glided well through the water. He began to feel uncomfortable and something inside him contracted and he sucked in water through the top of his head. He was immediately wracked with paroxysmal coughing and struggled to the surface. He decided he had to surface from time to time to breathe.

"I wonder how I'll be able to eat, and what," he thought.

As he swam on he heard the sound. It was singing, but unlike any he had ever heard before. He listened carefully and the melody seemed familiar, yet it was far, far different than anything he knew.

Jamie continued to swim toward the singing. As he got closer he recognized a bit of the melody. Where had he heard it before? He needed to hear more, so he increased his speed. The sound was louder now and he was able to put some of it together.

Could it be? Yes, yes it was the Shostakovich Fifth Symphony Largo, sort of, but how was it being sung? It was for an orchestra. How and what was singing it?

It must be Molli!

Jamie sped onward but the singing got no closer. Why was she swimming away? Why wasn't she swimming toward him? Finally he realized she did not know where he was. He would have to sing too. He tried, but ugly grunts were the only sounds he could produce. He kept swimming.

He had to keep coming up for air and it seemed to take too long to inhale. He tried to pull in more air and then he heard a sound. His Sound! A sort of whistle. If he could modulate his breathing, perhaps he could sing, as well. He tried and it worked. It didn't sound too good, but it was sound. He worked to make it louder and suddenly Molli's singing stopped.

He made more noise. It certainly didn't remind him of Shostakovich but it was noise.

A moment later he heard Molli again, and she was coming closer.

Closer.

Closer.

She was here!

They wound themselves around each other. It was pure joy! The feel of their sinuous bodies entwined with one another was joy beyond imagining. It was more than they had ever guessed it could be.

Quantum togetherness in Deerwhere was good.

Telepathic post-quantum entanglement in the Continuum of Minds was wonderful.

Entwining on Vodamesto was all that had gone before, with the purest ecstasy blended in.

m-ALERT #13
PRYNN'S VOYAGE
>>>Dated 0096 CE/CODE jwc<<<

Bethid, Master," Prynn, the uniale, questioned, "Why do I have to attend this Adoration Ritual? It's always the same and I feel absurd." Nes expression of distaste was stronger than the words.

"You are my Offspring; you must be there to prove my life is everlasting through you." Bethid, the Master, answered the adult uniale, and never wavered in looking directly at nem. Bethid's eyes bored into Prynn's. There was no flicker of movement, no distraction to nes stare. "You are the miracle of my body! I have everlasting life because my clone grew within me. I am as I always shall be."

"Don't do that!" Prynn said sharply. "I hate it

when you stare at me and preach." Nhe moved about the vestibule, purposely looking away from the demanding parent. One fist began to rhythmically beat against nes thigh.

"I am only observing my child, reminding you of the duty you share to our people, our congregation." The older uniale looked over Prynn's shoulder to better see nemself in the mirror.

"I am not a child!" Prynn said sternly, turning to glare directly at Bethid.

The Master's voice was quickly modulated to be gentle and coaxing. Nhe never broke nes stare while pulling on the ivory brocade robe. "No, of course not. Parents always feel that way. Here, help me with the cape." Nhe held out a hand for assistance, gesturing towards the beaded cape hanging nearby.

This was all preparation for the formal Rite of Adoration. The Bethidite uniales were waiting to thank their inspired leader for saving them all these years since the Great Earthquake. There had been hardships and constant struggles for survival but the Master assured them with the promises of lasting life. Because of the miracle of epigenetics, they would live to have better days. The faithful were gathered in the small amphitheater of broken concrete slabs constructed years earlier as a tribute to their Master. The podium and concrete altar stone were centered for perfect viewing and pitched for perfect acoustics.

Prynn hesitated. This ceremony of dressing brought memories of all processions, walking slowly behind Bethid, between the adoring uniales. Prynn was just a toddler the first time he heard Bethid delivering a sermon at the center altar and nhe was frightened by the booming quality of voice to be heard no matter where nhe moved. It was a constant reminder of nes una's power to envelope participants in the fullness of the words. Into childhood, Prynn was included in the theatrics of events and became attractive to the flock of uniales who attended Ritual. Nhe was given a robe, without a cape, identical to Bethid. It was carefully tailored as nhe grew. Nhe would follow Bethid down the arena aisle with a solemn imitation of nes parent, a serious expression over folded hands. If nes young eye caught movement or sight of a fren, Prynn would interrupt nes serious march with a smile, a quirky face, or even a little jig. Nhe reveled in the attention given to nem through murmurs or muffled laughter. If Bethid should turn quickly, the little doppelganger would quickly resume the serious pose.

The Miracle child was a religious prodigy, a genetic replication, a duplicate of the Master. Gradually, Prynn's little distractions were scripted into the procession. Not too many, just an endearing child, not too few. The Miracle began losing nes own devotion with adolescence. Young frens drifted away. Parading around the compound while others worked and accomplished projects triggered Prynn's curiosity. Once, exploring the Master's room nhe came upon a cache of electronics that were totally dead. Most of the electronics in the compound were non-activated antiques. They were leftovers of another era. Only Bethid's quarters had electricity occasionally provided by an aging generator. Glass faced machines in this room were different. They were kept almost tomblike as if waiting to be turned on again. When nhe asked the Master about it, nhe was slapped and told to never invade Bethid's privacy. Slaps progressed to more harsh punishments and beatings for daring to question. Nhe still wondered but kept it to nemself. No one seemed able or willing to answer nem. Maturing, Prynn lost interest in scripted antics. As an adult, nhe followed the tedious canon laid out for nem but nhe was no longer afraid of the booming voice. Prynn grew in height and strength, and the beatings subsided.

As Bethid turned in front of the dressing mirror, smoothing a sleeve, nhe attempted to counter Prynn's reluctance. "Maybe it's time for you to have a cape! Not full length, of course, but one just to mid-thigh. That would be appropriate to my heir apparent." Nhe smiled at the suggestion and glanced back, to see Prynn's reaction.

The fully mature uniale bristled at the Master's words. "I do not *want* a cape! I do not *want* to be part of a self-aggrandizing ritual. I do not *want* to be a Prynnce or Prynncess." Prynn stated fiercely, almost a growl, nes body tense as nhe faced nes parent. Hands were clenched into fists but there was no tremble in nes frame. "I have put up with this charade all my life and I am sick of it! I am not a miracle and neither are you!"

The two uniales facing each other were mirrored images in identical robes. Only years separated the worn, old face from the strong visage opposite. Bethid's attempt to mask aging with a powder was cracking from the callous expression. Nes posture was weakened in comparison to the uniale in prime. With tightened teeth, Bethid exclaimed, "You are my clone! You are my Offspring! You are my bril! You are MINE. You are my self! You are MY miracle." Only a flash of fear stopped an instinctive slap to Prynn's face.

In those moments there was more than anger

between them. Prynn felt hatred for years of subservience to the Master and constant reminders of being the clone. The tension in nes jaw matched the stare returned to Bethid.

For the Master, there was the shock of rejection and explosive need to regain control.

Angrily, Prynn pulled off nes own robe, jammed it into a knot, and defiantly threw it in Bethid's face. "You can do the same with your 'appropriate cape!'"

Bethid struggled with the cloth, wadded the garment into a ball and screamed, "You genetic mongrel! You don't deserve my everlasting life! You aren't worthy of my genetic heritage! Rot, you crossbreed cur, rot!" With nes manicured fingernails, nhe ripped and tore the robe into shreds.

That epithet finalized Prynn's decision and nhe stormed out of the room, dressed in undergarments, shoving past uniale servants in the hallway who cowered and hurried away at the shock of the outbursts.

In nes chamber, Prynn quickly dressed in nes roughest clothes, a tunic and pants nhe had worn while learning the woods with Quolon, an old soldier devoted to Bethid. Quolon had also taught Prynn the "royal" form of combat for parade purposes only. Quolon's leadership of the uniale guard who protected the compound became integral training with Prynn's maturity.

Prynn stuffed a few more pieces of clothing and extra boots into a bag and checked the empty hallway leading to the outside. Hurrying to exit, Prynn was surprised when Quolon stepped from an alcove to block nes escape.

"Out of my way!" Prynn instructed Quolon, using the tone always used with servants. Prynn did not want to shove past the faithful retainer, but the old uniale would not budge. Quolon was wearing the ceremonial garb for the Ritual. Nes wrinkled baldness glistened with nervous sweat.

"You can't leave, you are the Miracle!" Quolon's face was resolute without any sign of affection for the uniale nhe had tutored since birth. With each attempt Prynn made to sidestep, nhe was blocked.

"Sorry, old fren," Prynn said, and slammed the uniale aside. Quolon grappled with nem in a futile attempt of restraint. The old uni could not control one in prime and Prynn shoved nem at the wall then watched sadly as Quolon collapsed with an explosion of breath and slid down to the floor. Prynn looked at nes parent's servant and bit nes lip but turned and moved quickly toward the exit doorway.

Crossing the compound Prynn heard the hum of the faithful from the open theatre. The Ritual Procession had begun, it would keep the Bethidites occupied while nhe escaped to the woods.

ΔΔΔ

Prynn clambered over broken concrete runways to find a way to the coast. Nhe believed there would be some trading there because Bethid, the Master, would have rich foods or clothing not available with the compound skills and produce. Sensing a direction, Prynn pushed through the forest vegetation, and followed streams always running downhill. After a day's fast trek and cold, misty night, nhe finally shoved some bushes aside to see an expanse of water, gently lapping against a beach. The breeze was fresh with an unfamiliar scent and the sound of the water's small, gentle waves was a welcome respite to nes anger. Nhe was hesitant to choosing direction but nes hunger made the decision. The meager foods nhe brought with nem had run out. Going northeast, nhe followed the beach, and nes aching stomach, until the sand curved to an inlet.

A trading settlement was fitted into a tiny harbor with small boats moored at primitive docks. A mixture of cut logs, rotted pilings, and assorted planks formed a pier and dock, quickly constructed for efficiency. There was none of the of the cracked concrete of the compound. A few boats looked hewn from logs, and were tied to the dock or overturned on the beach.

In comparison, Prynn was in awe of the large wooden vessel at anchor in the inlet and nhe stood near a piling staring. In clothes roughened and dirtied by nes escape, nhe looked like many of the other uniales working about. Nes expression of wonder set nem apart. The planks of the ship were sculpted into a smooth bottom. Three large poles grew like trees from the surface with a small house on the flat area beneath the poles. Fabric was wrapped around some cross branches, while a chain going down into the water held the vessel in place.

A sailor smelling of sea life, sweat, and salt, watched Prynn and stopped putting supplies into a dinghy. Nhe spoke over Prynn's shoulder. "Ne'er you ever seen a ship before?"

"Not like this one! The size of it... it's made of planks and wood and..."

The uniale behind scratched nemself under nes cap and said to the newcomer, "Once all the steel vessels rusted away, after The Big Quake, we went back to the wooden ships. You don't need a steel industry, just some trees to cut down, and you can build or repair a schooner. We've come up from Sanfwhere to find traders. Any fool could pilot one of those steel ships. It takes a brain to work the sails and this old ship has done us well."

"Sanfwhere? What's that?"

The sea going uniale laughed out loud, "You're an ignorant one aren't you? What did you do, run away from that sicko compound of jabbering lunatics down south of here? You wouldn't be the first!" Nhe scratched more vigorously.

"I am not a jabbering lunatic!" Prynn asserted. "Just ... not familiar with this type of... configuration."

"Rigging?" the sailor fitted in with a curious look.

"Yeah, rigging." Prynn said quickly.

On board the schooner, the Captain gave orders to cast off in between curses for the absence of a crewmem. Spying Prynn, the captain yelled across the water and demanded, "Can you sail a ship?"

Prynn yelled back, with confidence. "Yes, I can!" Nhe believed nhe COULD sail a boat, though nhe never HAD sailed a boat. Nhe smelled an aroma coming from the cookhouse on the deck and truly wanted to sail in that ship.

The Captain yelled to the mate, "Bendixsen, check the uni out!" The few crew on the dock became very busy inspecting the mooring lines while furtively watching the scene with the newcomer. Taking Prynn's hands, the mate, Bendixsen, turned them over and Prynn could feel cracked skin roughing nes own. "Hhumpf" was all that was said but there was an old salt's suspicion of Prynn's soft hands, clothes, and demeanor. Nhe threw a hunk of line to Prynn saying, "Tie a bowlin' on a bight."

Without hesitation, Prynn tied one of the few knots nhe knew—used on the cincture of a robe. It would have to suffice. The strands were interlaced with all the showmanship Prynn could manipulate on the windy dock. Casually, nhe tossed the knot back to the mate, but the enticement from the cook house smoke was all nhe could think about.

The seafarer looked at the knot, turned it in nes fingers, and wondered what it was. It was unlike any tie used on the ship, but nhe was loathe to expose nes own ignorance. It was close enough! Nhe nodded to the Captain and waved the knot. With the tide changing, the wind coming up, and the original mariner missing, necessity made the Captain signal "Yes" to choose the agile bodied uniale before nem. "You're on, we'll try you out or kick you off at the next port." The mate kept the knot but gestured Prynn to get in the dinghy.

Before the Captain could change nes mind, Prynn followed the rest of crew as they got into the little boat. Lines were cast, oars were taken up. In just a few days, Prynn had transferred from being an icon in Bethid's Compound to rowing a boat towards a wooden vessel with strangers.

With a surprise eagerness, Prynn returned to nes lifetime habit of imitating the Master and following directions. The others in the dinghy picked up oars, Prynn picked up the ones remaining. Watching them, nhe arranged the oars so nhe wouldn't hit theirs. This would be easy, nhe thought. But when they started rowing towards the ship, Prynn was not in rhythm, nor used to the force needed to bend and pull. Nhe struggled to dip the oars in time and pull back while the others smirked, recognizing nes inexperience. So intent did nhe become, Prynn did not notice those behind nem had rested their oars and nhe alone was rowing. When the ship was replaced with a view of the shore, then the ship again, nhe stopped and turned to see the three sailors holding in their laughter. Nhe had been rowing in a circle.

"I hope you can sail a ship better than row a dinghy or we'll never get out of this inlet," Bendixsen said, again scratching nemself.

The feeling of a face flushed with embarrassment was new to Prynn so nhe bent more intently to the oars in hand. Reaching the ship, nhe saw a ladder of rope between nem and the deck railing. Climbing the rope ladder to get on board was easier than the rowing, although nhe was sure the one sailor remaining in the dinghy was shaking and twisting the ropes to put nem off balance.

Arriving on deck, nhe imitated the acknowledgement of the other sailors to the Captain and started to walk to the cookhouse. A rough hand grabbed nes arm, "Where ya going? There's work waiting before ya eat."

Startled by someone touching nem, Prynn tensed. Remembering where and why nhe was here, nhe paused. "Yes..." nhe wasn't sure of a title for a sea-going uniale.

"Aye, SIR!" Bendixsen answered. "On this ship, the respect of 'sir' goes for every uniale, woman, or man. Except for you. You haven't earned any respect."

"Aye, Sir!" The former Miracle answered and began imitating regimen of casting off. When ready, the anchor was raised and Prynn found the rhythm of circling the capstan easy to follow because of the chanty they all began. Nhe didn't know the words, but soon learned them because of their repetition. The voices were strong and melodious and all the small crew participated. Except the Captain. Prynn noticed the Captain only hummed to nemself and only when content with the crew's actions.

When the cook finally signaled, the other hands all preceded Prynn. Nhe was shoved aside as the newbie and by the time nhe sat at the rugged table there was only a small bowl of labskaus left. Prynn didn't hesitate or wait for a servant to serve nem, nhe scooped the warm stew gratefully into nes mouth. Nhe had never tasted anything so delicious.

Nancy, the cook, smiled at the gusto shown a rather mundane meal and scraped a little more out of the metal pot on the stove for the new crewmem. She was a buxom woman who moved about the small galley with the grace of a dancer. Her gray hair was pulled back by a cord. The apron tied around her waist had its bib pinned to an ample bosom. No gesture or action was wasted and all the crew was fed.

Prynn was surprised with the desire nhe felt to fit into the new role of a deckhand on a wooden vessel sailing around the remains of the Northwest Sound. Nes anger at Bethid and the compound left no alternatives and nhe deserted them. There had been no plans, no goals except escape. As much as nhe disdained being a Miracle child, nes pampered lifetime encoded habits nhe had to recognize and break in this new role. Nhe kept expecting others to wait upon nem and quickly learned it was not going to happen. Nancy scrapping stew scraps into nes bowl was as close as service came. There were no drones on board to do nes bidding, no uniale servants to care for nes clothing and personal needs, no congregation to adore nes slightest accomplishment.

The first night humbled nem as nhe was shown nes hammock in the hold. Perhaps it was originally ivory colored, but it was stained with sweat, dirt, and urine. Ragged lines tied it to the bulkhead, darkness covered the focsle. The crew watched tentatively. Determined, Prynn grabbed the foul smelling fabric and swung legs and torso up into the bag as nhe imagined it was done. With a rip, the rag shredded and tore away crashing Prynn to the deck in a heap.

Prynn lay crumbled, trying to withhold the rage within. The laughter of the others made nem want to lash out, to destroy them all. Nhe didn't move. Nhe tried to control nes breath. The laughter subsided, and a toe poked nem gently.

"Is nhe dead?" one whispered.

Now containing nes anger, Prynn rolled over, very slowly, and smiled broadly. Nhe looked directly at the crew, never wavering. Nhe was putting on a show of uniale control. The practice of growing up with Bethid allowed nem to compartmentalize feelings. Nhe kept on smiling.

That was the last thing the crew expected and they began to shuffle about, nervously excusing themselves until Bendixsen reached out a hand and pulled Prynn up. Appraising the uniale, nhe said, "Okay, that's enough. You can join us in the crew's quarters."

Prynn straightened up and answered, "Aye, Sir." Lanterns were lit, gestures made, and the rest of the night was spent in an almost comfortable bunk listening to the snores of nes crewmates. Nhe wanted a different life, and now that nhe started it, Prynn would make it happen.

The sailing was exhausting to Prynn even though they were short hauls. Muscles strained under new demands and the constant movement beneath nes feet. Nhe watched, listened, and took whatever work assigned. The crew accepted nem because of nes attitude and appreciation for the vessel.

The ship was designed to maneuver where larger ships would fail and yet have a capacity for good tonnage of cargo. The wooden vessel made from Douglas Fir was amazing to Prynn. At the Compound, buildings were larger but were ruins of concrete and blocks. The relic building could do little beyond crumble with age. The vessel was a moving entity, creaking and groaning, alive with possibilities as she sailed. Definitely, a ship was referred to as "she" even with the name "The Hyde." Prynn watched the details of every crew member until nhe could scamper where needed, tie the appropriate knot, or rig the proper line. Getting "sea legs" and "riding the ship" was more difficult to balance. On one blustery night, the crew was entertained by nes runs to the side of the ship to vomit. "Hmmmmm, chum." Was all Captain said.

The ship usually dropped anchor at dusk because the shoreline became so black, sightings were impossible. When first assigned night watch, Prynn anticipated a long boring night, doing nothing just like listening to one of Bethid's Sermons. It became a far different experience for nem. The Sound overcast shut out possible astronomical navigation. Sounds of landslides became common as the Sound settled into its new shape. On the clear nights, the stars were magnificent reminders of Prynn's freedom from Bethid, and nhe would take the watch with pleasure. Nhe had occasionally seen the mountain volcano from the Compound but it was not spectacular and usually hazy. One particularly bright night aboard the Hyde, with the full moon glistening on its snow, "the Mountain" gave Prynn answers to questions nhe never knew were there.

The excitement of being aboard the ship gave Prynn the experience of the wind versus calm, constant leaning to balance and a sense of wetness even when totally dry. Nhe savored the sounds of the night. Instead of repetitious mantras about Bethid, nhe heard the melodies of whales. The crew said that the whales in the Sound traveled in family pods and sang differently from the ones at sea. One crisp and clear night, Prynn was on the bow and saw an Orca, a killer whale, breach in the moonlight, white and black markings rotating above the dark water. The power to lift such a body up and totally out of the water amazed nem. In the background, the volcano mountain shimmered under its snowfall cape. It was only a few seconds, but it would be lifelong in nes memory.

ΔΔΔ

With the cold night wind, two of the mates joined Prynn trying to warm nemself by the cast iron stove in the cookhouse. Nhe had been on night watch and finally succumbed to the temptation of some hot tea. The others, Mack and Jack, were just searching if any food was left out from dinner. No one on the crew was sure which uniale was Jack or Mack but they were together so much, it didn't really seem to matter what to call them. They both would answer to either name. They were both ship's carpenters while sharing the necessary bag of tools.

"How's it going?" Jack or Mack asked while nibbling a crust of hard tack.

"All right, I'll finish watch soon." Prynn answered. Nhe rubbed hands together before putting them back in the fingerless gloves. The other crew had given nem their few clothing leftovers suitable for the rigors of the water. Prynn appreciated that these uniales had little to share but still did. Nhe was dressed in mismatched tunic and pantaloons, far different from a beaded robe and there was no cape in sight. The watch cap had a few moth holes but someone had woven twine to cover them. The cap was vital to a bald uniale. A scent of working sweat permeated the clothes but Prynn was becoming accustomed to it as nes own was blended.

"Jack, I've been thinking about Nancy," Prynn said, trying to use the quiet hour to satisfy curiosity. "Isn't it kind of weird to have one woman on a ship of uniales? I mean, she's a good cook, but it must be difficult to be without her own kind." Prynn wondered how many women were in the trading business.

Jack and Mack nodded mischievously behind Prynn's back. "Has no one told you Nancy's story?"

"Nancy and Nettle?" the two moved even closer to Prynn and spoke in low tones, warming themselves in the darkened galley. "Before the Big Quake, people started looking around for transportation. SanFwhere was in terrible shape, and there were some who wanted to break Confederation Quarantine. The Cap'n and some people from a museum got to looking at old sailing ships and restored some of the ships at the pier. But that's another story." Mack could sense nhe was losing Prynn's attention.

"Anyway," Jack hurried on, "The Cap'n was great friends with Nettle who helped refit the wood schooner and wanted him to be mate but Nettle was newly married and wouldn't leave his bride behind. Even though most of their trips up and down the pacific coast would only be a few weeks, and Nettle could visit her often. It warn't like those Ocean trips that could take months or even the codfishing trips that meant 6 months at sea. So, the Cap's said any man that devoted should bring his wife along. She was a good worker, started as a deck hand then moved up to cook. We were at sea when the Big Quake hit... Oh, about Nancy. You know, she's all about the ship but there's something sad about her. She's a widow woman. Once she lost her husband, Nettle, as fine man and sailor as you'd meet, she stayed married only to the sea."

"Well, you got to go back right after the Great Earthquake. We were still able to ship out of SanFwhere colony although getting out of harbor and through the debris of the big rusty bridge was pretty rough. We were going south to look for other survivors, you know, settlements and such. Only recent we came north. The Cap'n figured there was real possibilities for trade for a good ship and crew," began Mack.

Without a pause, Jack continued. "We saw the damnest things. There was always people living outside the Confederation, but that quake stirred 'em all up, threw 'em around and made 'em desperate. One place we anchored, the Cap'n was real careful about bringing the ship into a port. Instead, we always dropped anchor and just took a dinghy ashore. This one time, Nancy and her husband Nettle were with us and there was a miserable pack of people all sharing some kind of sickness I'd never seen in all my years at sea." Nhe looked to nes mate and asked, "You ever seen enything like that?"

"Naw, never! They was coughing and had sores and looked like they was burning up their eyeballs. We din stay long, just got some fresh water up above the settlement and scurried back to the ship."

Mack took up the narrative again, "But it was long enough for poor ol' Nettle to catch the fever. For days on the ship, nhe was sick and pukin' and Nancy took care of him as best she could. In fever, Nettle kept calling out, 'Don't Leave Me! Don't leave me!' He'd not let Nancy out of his sight. 'Don't Leave me!' We'd hear him screaming til his strength give out. 'Don't leave me...' No matter what Nancy did, she couldn't stop the fever and he upped and died." Solemnly, nhe paused, out of respect to the dead. "We sewed Nettle in a hammock and buried him at sea."

"Yeah, it was a right good passing the Cap'n gave him, and Nancy cried a bit. She said she mourned the only man she ever loved and she watched as long as she could as Nettle sank beneath the waters. We respect her for that. And oh, it's his watch cap you're wearing."

Prynn squirmed uneasily, nes hand reaching toward the cap now pressing ominously on nes scalp.

Mack and Jack moved closer to Prynn, shading nem from the light of the coals in the stove.

Jack whispered, "That's when it started."

"What?" Prynn was surprised that nhe was also whispering. Nes hands kept inching to nes cap.

"The creaking, and worse. The scratching."

Prynn could barely hear nem. The moist night cold seeped back into nes hands as the quiet surrounded the three hunkered near dying embers in the black stove.

"The scratching?" Prynn asked, hardly breathing.

"We'd hear it at night. Scratching. Scratching like fingers raking themselves on the hull of the ship. Sometimes the sound is the splitting of wood fragments like something ripping away the planks."

"But that's not as bad as the wailing" Mack whispered. Nes voice thinned out to repeat the begging...   "Don't leave me. Don't leave me! Over and over again."

"Don't... leave... me... "

"Don't... leave... "

"Don't... "

With a whoop, Mack and Jack burst out laughing so hard and loud they fell on top of Prynn who was still mesmerized by the tale. Nhe gulped some air and shoved the two of them away. Nhe didn't know whether to punch them in anger or join the hilarity. They had conned nem! The miracle performer had fallen for a ghost story! Watching their mirth and belly laughs, Prynn finally had to laugh at nemself.

After night watch, rocking gently in nes bunk, Prynn was amused at nes gullibility. Nhe never thought of the rough sailors as having a humorous side. Nhe wondered how nhe could return the prank. Drifting to sleep, nhe heard the planks scratching beneath nem. Like fingers clawing at the wood in the bilge. With bated breath, nhe waited for a plaintive cry, "Don't... leave... Me."

ΔΔΔ

At the next small community, Prynn worked lines aboard ship while waiting for a turn to row to shore. The settlement on the water's edge was not much to look at but it was land and there were people milling about as if it was a holiday. Nhe realized, it really was something special. Settlements along the Sound were tenuous since the Great Quake. A few permanent docks were set up if possible and they served the fishing boats. Most populace lived farther inland on farms and they would travel to the shores on the occasion of a trading ship. It was a spectacle for a ship like the Hyde dropping anchor. The three masted schooner was a sight to show the children. For decades from the Confederation years of quarantine, through the Computer Shut Down and finally, the Great earthquake, ships were only myths. Now, a bona fide wooden sailing ship was anchoring to trade goods and connect the isolated peoples with a whole world.

On the dock, hefting containers, Prynn almost felt like the celebrity nhe had been in Bethid's procession. That had been false adoration, but this was real. Real people, working farmers, trading with a real crew. Children ran about, in most people's way, but parents encouraged them to watch what was happening. Bendixsen soon had an audience, telling them about the Hyde, where it came from, where it was going. " The 156 foot length and 36 foot breadth of this ship was created out of the forests that grow right to the sea. You could build your own ships here... if you knew how. The baldheaded masts, at 106 feet, were rigged to be easily worked by a small crew." Nhe gestured at the masts to give the onlookers time to crane their necks.

The Captain and Nancy took care of the trading,

mostly barter. No one had any currency to share.

"Hey Captain, any chance to take the young ones on the boat? They's sure t'be thrilled," said one tall man with a healthy beard. A younger man next to him nodded in agreement.

"Not boat!" the Captain retorted, brusquely, "The Hyde's a schooner, a ship. What do you have to trade?"

The man, called Deenam by others, held up some metal tools. "This axe head has been recently sharpened and has a good weight to it. The hammer is carefully hafted into its wooden handle and polished. You could trade 'em for something else along the line."

The Captain started to walk on but looked at the eager faces and nodded. "Well, tools always have value. We'll take em. Give 'em to Prynn at the dinghy."

The children scampered toward the little boat and Prynn noticed the man fidgeting. He wanted to go too as did the young man called Owen, evidently in the family. Looking at the men and children, the captain nodded once more, while Deenam and the youngsters climbed carefully in beside Prynn. They pressed together to allow room for Owen and Prynn laughed but didn't object. Rowing the boat back to the ship, Prynn noticed the older man looking at nem strangely. Probably just the excitement of a boat ride. Prynn took some time to guide the visitors around the ship, to soak up the awe they expressed that was so like nes own. "And here's where the crew eats, be careful, that stove is always hot... here's the anchor chain... now, down in the hold... " Prynn wanted to show everything but a call from the Captain brought the tour to a close.

Deenam handed the young ones over the railing to Owen waiting below. Again, he stood with an inquisitive look at Prynn. Pausing for a moment, he asked Prynn, "Don't I know you?"

"Don't know how you could, I'm new to the crew." Prynn said while urging the older man back down the rope ladder into the dinghy. The man shook his head, then attended to the excited children. "Owen, settle your son down, you don't want to tip us over." He watched Prynn row all the way back to shore and shook his head as the group landed. He just couldn't place the memory.

With just a few days of successful trading, the ship finished loading items into its hold including a goat that Nancy insisted would be a good investment. They had some salted fish, tools, and lumber planks that were fit to make barrels. A blacksmith was able to let go of precious nails for a better bellows. The hold was evened out. There was even a small area for Nancy's goat, with extra potatoes and hay available. The anchor was hoisted, the crowd waved, As the Hyde moved out to new anchorage in the Sea, Prynn thought nhe heard someone from shore yell out, "Beware of the pirates!" Nhe was too intent on raising the spinnaker sail to pay attention.

Prynn felt an unusual contentment that night. Discouraged by life at the Compound, nhe appreciated the companionship of the crew and the value of their lives on the ship. The ship. More than a design constructed of wood, it had become shelter, a home, and a link to people and faraway places. Nes life was now cleaved into two parts, Before the Ship and On the Ship. Before, in all activities of the Compound, Prynn had never imagined shifting cargo in a rocking hold, sighting whales frolicking alongside the foaming waters, or hearing sea lions honk warnings. Before, nhe never realized the emotions of these last days. On ship, there had been companionship and even terror. There was the dread of sailing around the Sound at night with overcast, no stars, night tides, and sounds of earth slides. Fear that knotted the stomach and buckled the knees was foreign to Prynn until "On ship"—fear was experienced and overcome.

Redemption. What did that word mean? Is that what the Hyde meant to nem? Prynn would have to think about it or find another to express nemself. Then again, nhe didn't know how to define an idea in the world such as theirs. As always, questions led to more questions until another word came to mind, "Promises." The uniale was genetically designed to be the third human, and they were more than just promises.

ΔΔΔ

Sailing the Sound had meant going into inlets and straights, anchoring in deep water and visiting assorted people along the shore. Prynn heard another name for the inland waters, the Salish Sea. It was an ancient name but seemed to appeal to the crew for soon they were all using the name, even the Captain. Landfall was made when water was needed and once, Mack and Jack went hunting to fetch fresh meat for Nancy's culinary arts. Prynn was settling into a comfortable berth with no regrets for abandoning Bethid's domain.

Another night watch, the ship was rocking more heavily than usual. Then Prynn heard the thumping at the side of the vessel. Thump. Thump. It was followed by a scratching sound like hands on the planks and undiscernible whispers. Prynn grinned at Mack and Jack trying to get nem scared of a ghost. Nhe stepped quietly down from the prow and moved in the dark to catch nes crewmates. As nhe eased toward the starboard side, nhe stopped suddenly, becoming rigid. It was not Mack and Jack playing a prank. It was not crew silently climbing over the railing. Three strangers with weapons in their hands were boarding the ship!

Prynn yelled "HALT!' And grabbed for the ship's bell. Nhe was able to get two clangs of alarm before one figure slammed a fist into nes stomach, knocking the wind out of nem and crashing Prynn to the deck. On the deck, Skip, the terrier, was barking frantically biting at the intruders' legs. Gasping, Prynn lunged forward into the adversary ramming the hulk back into the other two on deck who immediately jumped on Prynn's back. With three strangers holding and punching nem, Prynn was collapsing to the deck when nhe heard the scream of a banshee. It was Nancy in her apron with her cast iron skillet swinging and smashing it into one head with a thunking sound, a collapsing victim, and spurts of blood. Circling the second attacker, she vied to swing again.

The other figure dropped Prynn and yanked Nancy by the hair until she screamed and swung the skillet back over her head with both hands to crash into the assailant behind her. Mack and Jack came out of the forecastle alarmed by the mayhem on deck as Prynn twisted away from the holding arms, grabbed a belaying pin and crashed it into the skull nearest nem. A fourth and fifth brigand had leapt over the railing, and Mack slammed into one while Jack wrestled the last intruder to the deck. The figure tried to escape and Prynn pounded the face with a fist. When that failed to stop the fighting creature, Prynn grabbed the collar and beat the uniale head into the deck. Nhe didn't stop until the crushed skull was bleeding in nes hands.

Prynn jumped up to see the rest of the crew containing the brigands. Nhe was breathing heavily and thought nes heart was going to split nes chest. Nhe grabbed the belaying pin again and wavered to find another combatant but the Captain and Bendixen were forcefully holding the intruders together, bloodied or not. Nancy stood by with her skillet and Jack had a carpenter's sledge. Prynn could not calm down. Every part of nem was ready to fight on even though there was no one left to fight. Nhe trembled and went to Nancy and Mack and Jack and saw they were in the same state of excitement. Nancy kept nervously swinging the skillet by her side as if she would hit anyone else who provoked her.

"That's enough, everybody. Calm down. We've got them." the captain said giving an extra hard punch to the closest brigand. Nes voice was a command and it slowed the excitability of the crew. In the darkness, the wounds of the assailants were not clear but their moans and the stickiness of the deck gave the battle to the crew of the Hyde. Skip growled for emphasis.

"You stinking assholes! You dare board my ship!" The Captain yelled with emotion never seen before. Nhe slammed another blow into the one intruder still standing, then motioned towards the little boat that had allowed such intrusion. With a nod from the Captain, Jack disappeared then pulled up a ballast rock from the hold and crashed it down on the little boat, smashing through its bottom to let dark water pour into it. "Well, you like the water so much you can swim in it!" The Captain released and hefted the first pirate over the railing and into the water below. The crew followed their captain's example and in the night they could hear the splash of bodies, the gargle of water.

Bendixen cut the painter line holding their sinking boat to the ship. The beaten swimmers tried to catch the boat pieces but the sounds and cries meant only a few reached it. The frigid water of the Salish Sea began claiming its own.

"You did good, Prynn!" The Captain pounded Prynn on the back. "We've taught those pirates to deal with the Hyde Crew. Everyone, come to my cabin, there's grog to settle your nerves.!"

In the captain's quarters, surrounded by the crew, Prynn felt exhilarated. Prynn was no petulant child throwing a robe at a parent, nhe was an adult uniale who defended home and family against marauders, with strength. Nhe had been in danger, faced it with quick thinking, engaged an enemy physically. Whether it was genetics or a lifetime of suppressed anger, Prynn was euphoric.

ΔΔΔ

The weather made perfect sailing for the Hyde. There were villages along the coast with their makeshift docks for the ship's dinghy to land. Sculpted canoes hauled goods out to the ship at anchor. The pilot who guided the ship into the southern waters left the crew at one village and another was recruited to safely traverse north. The Great Earthquake had redesigned the shoreline, the debris was gradually clearing itself, the rains and sunshine beckoned to the wildlife, and people were able to use the great waterway for commerce and communication. There were more fishing villages and people familiar with the Salish Sea. The fears of pandemics and contamination which separated them for centuries were broken into the needs of survival.

Prynn was on watch one foggy morning when nhe saw a cluster of tall angles and geometric shapes on the eastern shore. The moist air and gentle rocking of the ship kept nem from identifying the ghosts.

"It was a great city, centuries ago," Bendixsen's voice murmured to the unasked question. "Before the wars, before the Pandemics, even before the Confederation, it was bustling with men and women and computers and commerce and vehicles and art and learning."

"Centuries?" Prynn asked. "What happened?"

"Oh...   wars,   overpopulation, Pandemics, Confederation, computers, vehicles." There was a wry tone to the words.

"And it was just left to rust?" Prynn questioned. Even Bethid's compound was being used, nhe thought. Why wasn't the city?

"I don't know, I wasn't there. SanFwhere was the same way. People just left it to move on to other places. The cities were just too much maintenance, I guess." Nhe chuckled and fingered the smooth wood of the railing. As the schooner slipped by the city skeleton one more thought occurred. "Maybe humans just need to keep moving, trying new things. Looking for new land. It seems to be one gene that's never been deleted." Another chuckle and Prynn was left alone on deck to nes own thoughts.

As the early sun filtered through the thinning fog, Prynn tried to imagine the city at its peak. Nhe couldn't.

There wasn't enough information in nes mind to imagine the visuals of a live city. Nhe reached down and petted Skip, now on deck and looking for attention. Prynn had shared a few bits of biscuit with the terrier and was officially accepted as crew by the little dog. The little Skipper's world consisted of this ship, a ship that was taking Prynn to the rest of the world!

The ship rounded a cliff of rock and soil that hid their view of hills to the east. This escarpment formed by the great earthquake was still adjusting and sculpting itself. Prynn saw waterfalls and rivulets that escaped from the lake forming above. A small trading post on the Sea was the only obvious access to the land beyond. It was all that remained of the former colony of Deerwhere, now flooded and deserted. Traders there had crops from a distant farm including some jugs of wine. Prynn accompanied the Captain and Nancy to the shore. The Captain was humming to nemself in anticipation of good trading.

Offered a sample of the potatoes and greens, the Captain asked to taste the fermented grapes obviously being held back.

"Oh, Captain, this is Knight's best quality wine. It is a premium and we don't have too much to trade. It's hard to get large amounts transported here from Rook's Farm. You know, the Quake and all tore up the trails but we're working on some new roadways. We've got draft animals to pull the wagons we're making and soon we'll be able to haul larger quantities of all our trade here to put in your hold." The farmer extolling the wares was putting all effort to making a future deal with the Ship's Captain.

The Captain's eyes partially closed as nhe savored

the flavors and aromas of the liquid. "Here, Nancy, take a sip. What do you think?" A mug passed between them.

"It'll do." Nancy said non-committedly. She had traded enough to know emotions were never demonstrated.

More bartering followed more sipping, more denying, more pledging and possible exchanges. Prynn was busy taking goods back and forth between the ship and shore and laughed to nemself at the posturing and discussion of the traders on the temporary landing. Once, rowing to the shore, nhe heard angry words and thought Nancy would whip out her skillet to bonk the farmer on the head. By next landing, all were happy and shaking hands.

"Prynn!" called the Captain. "Bring some of those redwood planks we have in the hold. By the time we return, these farmers might have a proper cooper to make them into barrels. Then we can really talk trade."

As the whole crew returned to the ship, the farmer waved a cheery hand and called out, "Give Greetings to Noral and Savot at Ever. Tell them we made a lovely trade with you!"

Trade from small boats and canoes followed the wine acquisition. The crafts would come alongside and goods would be exchanged on the deck. The hold was re-packed to accommodate different weights of cargo. It was getting tight for Nancy to access her goat for milking but the cheeses she pressed guaranteed the crew would leave an aisle clear for her.

The approach to Ever was very difficult. The Pilot picked up to guide them had boasted more knowledge than nhe possessed. There were false starts and the resetting of sails. The Captain was furious and ordered soundings. Finally, nhe guided the ship nemself. The sea bottom was jagged into rips of sediment. The anchor was not dropped until the Captain believed it to be safe and then nhe physically threw the pilot into the first landing boat. Prynn was surprised that the pilot was flung into a boat!

ΔΔΔ

Prynn recognized a basic layout design of the Ever Streets. There was a stark similarity to the grid of Bethid's Compound but softened with additional small structures and greenery. A former docking area was damaged too much to accommodate large vessels. It was modified to allow small boats to dock. There was even a wooden sign with the city name of EVER carved into it. The gathering of structures bore little resemblance to the skeleton city passed by the Hyde. It was a ghost. Here, Prynn sensed a bustling, growing excitement. In Ever, humans were more than surviving, they were thriving.

Too occupied with taking goods back and forth to the ship, it wasn't until the second day in port that Prynn was able to go ashore. Nhe was given permission by the Captain to explore the little city. Nhe was surprised at nes initial wobbliness walking away from the dock. Nhe gradually regained "land legs" and walked through little alleys and stopped to look in a shop display.

"Adrion! What are you doing here?" A stranger came from behind, slapping Prynn roughly on nes back and swinging Prynn around. There was a huge smile on nes face.

Tensed, Prynn turned quickly to the uniale, hands

in fists by nes side. Since the confrontation with the pirates, nhe was wary. Nhe faced the stranger's smile with a stern look.

"Oh, sorry... I thought you were someone else!" The uniale quickly looked at Prynn's mismatched clothing and mended watch cap and released nes grip. Nhe held up open hands and backed away, saying "Excuse me." Nes confused expression continued with another, "Sorry!"

Prynn watched the stranger leave and realized this was the second time nhe had been mistaken. At the Compound, Prynn was the Miracle. No one could mistake Prynn for anyone but Bethid's Bril. On ship, the small crew was their own community. Prynn smiled to nemself and added one more experience to nes ditty bag.

That evening, the crew was invited to dinner with citizens of Ever. Bendixen chose to stay on board with Skipper, but Nancy, Jack, and Mack, and Prynn were glad for the diversion and followed the Captain. They were greeted at the landing and escorted to a grassy parkway. Prynn had expected a dining area but instead there was a landscaped depression. Centered within the valley, a plaza of small stones radiated out from a huge pile of wood. It was a firepit as Prynn had never seen. Around a mound of carefully stacked wood, a circle of stones created a safe plaza. Small colored stones were fitted like decorative tiles in a pattern of a sun burst spreading from the fired center. Coral, scallops, various sea skeletons were integrated into the design. The person next to Prynn saw nes fascination and offered, "Each of the stones was delivered by hand from the people of Ever. It gave them a partnership with the design."

Enclosing the outer edge of the mosaic was a low

bench for seating with more benches terraced to accommodate additional people. Prynn thought how different it was to have people interacting with each other. At the compound, everything was designed for Bethid's ego.

In the shadows there was a table with plates of food that could be eaten casually, without services and utensils. Waiting near the table were older uniales who introduced themselves as Savot, the historian, Noral and Kalen, and others. It was difficult to know their ages because they were bald like most uniales. From the respect others demonstrated, they must have been elders of the group. They made little attempt to hide their confusion when the Captain introduced the Hyde's crew. It was as if they could not take their eyes away from Prynn

Prynn was used to being the center of attention with Bethid but the stares nhe received here made nem pause. Nhe stood tall, ignored the shabbiness of nes sailor garb, and followed the others. Watching the citizens, and the gestures of welcome, nhe imitated their serving themselves. There were no drones waiting upon them as there had been at the Compound. A few attendants assisted the diners and later joined them seated on logs or benches around the wood pile.

When all were seated, Noral stood and placed a torch on the carefully prepared wood. Almost immediately, the wood and tinder burst into a bonfire with sounds of approval from the gathering. Almost a prayer followed as the gathered people repeated, "Pietas--Officium—Constantia—Aequum—Gravitas—Tria in Aeternum." A simple blessing, for a Joyful Life.

Savot, rose to speak, and nes voice was warm and

sincere. Nhe wore a helmet that may have been electronic at one time but now seemed to be ceremonial or token of status. The stares of the elders became intermittent as they divided their attention between their meal and listening. "Welcome, welcome Captain and Crew of the Hyde. We are so glad of your visit and want to hear all about your voyage from SanFwhere. Your ship is magnificent, and we hope it will lead to more trade and exchanges between our peoples.

Prynn was not used to the boisterous talk surrounding the people balancing their food in hand. Nhe and Bethid had always dined alone with a minimum of "discussion". To Bethid, discussion meant repeating the wonderment of nemself and nes running the compound. To Prynn, it had simply meant boredom.

"Where is Adrion?" Someone called out and as the uniales looked about for the missing uniale, Noral said humorously "Oh, he's probably off somewhere fighting cougars." The Ever people laughed at the well-known joke.

Not to be left out, Prynn interposed—"Who is Adrion? What cougars?"

Savot said hastily, "Adrion is Noral's offspring. It was nes birth years ago that led to the reprogramming of the Deerwhere computer. It's a long story, we'll tell you sometime but now, enjoy the crab cakes. And don't worry about cougars, Adrion will keep them in hand." Nhe shook nes head with a knowing smile and turned the conversation back to the Captain. Talk and banter continued while the captain answered questions about Sanfwhere and the communities surrounding the Salish sea.

Prynn tried to insert a story about the Bethid

Compound but was stopped by Noral's warning look and statement "We know enough about the compound. We... came across it... after the earthquake and have no desire to revisit it." Nes disparaging tone was final.

Quickly, Kalen changed the subject to recount how Deerwhere populace had moved to Ever. Nes eyes moved quickly around the table to include everyone. "We restarted our community here although we retain strong ties with Rook's Farm. Noral and our agricultural people used Rook's plant stock to start our farms here. With climate changes, and earth adjustments, we're proud of food production!"

Goodbyes were being said as the firelight died, and coals began to glow. The scent of burning wood still hung in the air as the crew began to leave the clearing. People were milling about when the quiet, congenial atmosphere was suddenly exploded by the entrance of uniales dressed in hunting garb with weapons and a huge deer carried slung between poles. Laughing, gesticulating, the party called greetings and was received with humor from the diners.

Noral, so subdued during dinner, rose to hug the lead uniale, and spoke like the parent nhe was. "Adrion, you're a mess! Get that animal around to the kitchens. You others, as well! We're trying to be civilized here!" Nes words were a reprimand, but the pleasure and pride in nes smile was obvious. " How is the Reserve? Is there Balance?"

"All is well, The Reserve is in Aequum." Adrion responded. It was a mantra of assurance.

"Excellent! Now take yourselves to the kitchens." Turning to the Captain, Noral explained, "Ever has established a wild reserve that is seasonally re-balanced for conservation. It is an ongoing promise to our people."

The hunting party started to return toward the kitchens in the building complex with more laughter and awkwardness. The buck's head dangled while its haunches were jostled. The mayhem continued until the deer was repositioned for carrying and on the way to the kitchen. Forest debris from the soft boots traced the path.

Prynn began to exit but was stopped by Adrion's outstretched hand and direct eye contact. "Hello, I am Adrion. You may have heard of me."

"Oh, yes, I have." Prynn smiled as nhe took the extended hand to shake. The two appraised each other, holding the shake a bit longer. They were equal in height, but the muscular build of the hunter was fine-tuned while Prynn had been "a miracle" until the hard work of sailing the last months. Adrion was obviously a mature uniale compared to Prynn in Prime. They both had blended skin tones denoting a mixed background of genes. Adrion scanned the face of this new uniale with a look of curiosity. Then the moment passed. Prynn and the crew were given a torch and returned to the ship.

Thinking of the evening, Prynn was very aware that Adrion was a leader in Ever by nes own personality, being a cause for the uniale rebellion that shutdown a quantum computer, and from the myths that grew from nes passage after the Great Earthquake. Prynn had been declared a miracle, Adrion seemed to have earned that title on nes own.

In the days following the bonfire, socializing gave way to trading. The captain was particularly eager to obtain some of the great lumber near the coast. The tall straight firs particularly beckoned to be made into masts. Ready cut and roughly milled wood were loaded into the hull of the ship through the hatches on the rear deck. The Hyde crew laughed good naturedly as Adrion's team maneuvered small boats out to the anchorage to unload some lumber. Because it was an unusual sight, many of the townspeople came down to the landing to watch. One of them was Noral, watching carefully.

"Hey, you there! Prynn? Are you regular on the Hyde?" Noral called as Prynn landed the dinghy and was tying off on a bollard.

'Yes, that's right. I'm Prynn." Nhe thought it an unusual question since they had been introduced at the bonfire. There were not many strangers in town loading a ship. Who else could nhe be?

Noral moved near and eyed Prynn closely. "Who is your parent? Where are you from?" nhe asked bluntly.

"I'm from the Compound in the southern waters. I tried to tell you before but you wouldn't listen." Prynn resumed his work with the lines.

Noral grabbed Prynn's arm and said sternly, "Come to my quarters after your work." Prynn yanked nes arm away from this uni's grasp as Noral turned and called to Adrion who had been listening surreptitiously. "You, too, Adrion, come and bring Prynn." Nhe turned quickly and left the area. Prynn's glare at Adrion was returned in kind.

With the Captain's permission, Prynn strode beside Adrion that afternoon. Neither had much to say. Both wondered why they were beckoned.

Entering Noral's rooms, the elder motioned the visitors to sit. Prynn sat opposite Noral but Adrion stood behind nes una's chair watching Prynn intently. Without greeting or offering refreshment, Noral began. "Tell me again Prynn, whose Compound was your home? When were you born? Who is your uniale parent?"

Prynn felt old angers rising at the brusque manner of Noral's words. Nhe did not want to be interrogated for nes past, especially by a stranger. "Why do you want to know, elder?" Nes hands tightened into fists but nhe never took nes eyes from the uniales sitting opposite.

After a long silent stare, it was Noral who conceded, and glanced away. "I'm sorry, Prynn, for my rudeness. It's just... ." Nhe began again. "The spring of the Great earthquake, a party of us from Deerwhere traveled south, looking for help." Nhe looked up to Adrion, standing near and smiled a bit sadly at the memory. "It was Adrion's great adventure but there were mishaps as well. We—all the travelers—were held at the Bethid Compound. We escaped but there were consequences."

"Consequences! You call it consequences, Una, when you were raped, people were shot, and we had to escape being hunted in the forest?" Adrion's outburst shocked the others and nhe began to pace the small room. Nes anger built at the memory of finding Noral, of the threatening stance of the Compound leader, of Noral's long recovery. "Keeper's curse! That bag of Compound gowno deserved to be shot and a lot more if I'd had my way!"

Prynn went silent, nhe felt numbed by the words being thrown by Adrion. Was this the harsh ranting of a stranger or the other side of a story told all nes life? Where was the lie, the deception? With tightened jaw, Prynn faced the accuser and shouted, "What are you saying? I am Bethid's miracle, I am nes cloned self.".

"You are Bethid's Bastard! That's no miracle!" Adrion ground the words through clenched teeth. Nhe and Prynn both trembled with rage, paralyzed by the accusations.

"Stop it! Both of you! Stop!" Noral commanded with all the force within nem. Nes breathing was as ragged as the two uniales before nem but there was no doubt of nes authority. "Prynn, again, when were you born?"

Taking a breath, Prynn answered, "The winter following the Great Earthquake. That means nothing! Miracles don't have timetables." Prynn rationalized. Nes expression remained resolute as nhe grasped at the stories Bethid told.

"No," Noral agreed. "But they do have gestation tables. All a person needs to do is see the two of you together to know the genetics speak for themselves. Your appearance, your manner of movement, your facial expressions when you smile or frown." Nhe paused with a small grin. "Your tempers! Our Deerwhere gene pool was restricted by years of quarantine yet here you are, the image of Adrion. The image of me." The room became totally silent. Heavy breathing slowed. Anger drained away leaving exhaustion in its place. Hurtful words were silenced. Thoughts were muddled with confusion.

Prynn turned away, there was nothing left for nem to say. The recognition by other strangers along the voyage and the physical presence of Adrion in this small room convinced Prynn of Bethid's deceit and Noral's truth. Prynn was just a pawn in Bethid's plan, an artifact to Bethid's ego. Not a miracle. Prynn was a stolen bid for reproduction. Clarity. This encounter with a parent and half sibling gave clarity to Prynn's discontent.

Later. They would have to talk later. There was too much mystery, too many questions to be answered. Details needed to be processed and sorted. Prynn straightened nes shoulders, turned to the door, and determinedly left Noral and Adrion together as uniale and bril. About nemself, that would take more contemplation. Nhe returned to the dinghy and rowed to the ship. Crawling into the bunk, nhe could only identify nemself as Prynn, sailing mate of The Hyde.

ΔΔΔ

"Prynn ! Get up! You've got duty ashore." Jack or Mack shook Prynn awake after a night of fitful sleep. "The captain wants you to go with a land crew to get some mast timber and it means NOW!"

Grabbing some food at the galley, Prynn was still dressed in yesterday's clothes and nhe scrambled to get into a dinghy ready to be rowed to shore. Approaching the little dock, nhe saw Adrion already waiting with another uniale and a team of horses with a driver remaining up the pathway.

"Come on, little sibling! The day's waiting and your captain doesn't want it wasted!" Adrion reached down and grabbed Prynn's hand to yank nem onto the dock. Nes demeaner was totally different from the seriousness and anger in last night's meeting with Noral. Nhe even laughed at Prynn's expression of distrust.

"What are you saying, what have we to do together?" Prynn looked around quickly at nes mates but they seemed totally focused on securing the lines and avoiding nes eyes.

"Your Captain has eyes on some of our great timber. It would be a great trade product so we're going to the forest to fetch it, and you're coming with us to make sure we pick the best stand!" Adrion stared at the younger uni as if daring nem to object. "Come on!" Nhe slapped Prynn on the back and led the way to the horses without looking back. Nhe was used to nes directions being followed. At the cart, Adrion turned for a moment and grinned. Quietly, nhe said "We've got a lot to talk about, little bril."

"Don't call me that! I'm no one's little bril." Prynn answered sharply.

"Oh, we'll see about that, we'll see!"

The workday that followed allowed little time for personal discussions. Adrion's team with the horses led the way into deep forest. At some places, the horses had to struggle to drag the cart over rough terrain but Adrion had a definite goal in mind. The teams broke into a cut clearing that showed previous harvesting. Adrion's look of satisfaction showed pride in the vegetation as if nhe had cared for it nemself. Actually, nhe had, as the community conservationist.

"Here it is!" Adrion gestured to the rest of them, then sat on a cut stump. "Go to it, pick your trees and we'll cut them for you!" Nhe brought out a food package and offered it around to the land team. "Oh, sorry. I didn't bring any landlubber food for you, I thought you'd, some bring some sea salt or hard tack with you."

Mack and Jack mumbled to themselves then took Prynn's arm to pull nem toward the tree stand. "We'll eat later, here's some of the hard tack we brought." While Adrion's crew ate and watched, the three sailors moved into the stand and marked tall, straight, specimens with a cut X. All the trees were prime for trading as masts or beams or pillars.

"They're marked!" Prynn said returning to the clearing and stood looking down at Adrion. Nhe expected to casually watch the lumber cutting from the same stump Adrion now vacated. Instead, Adrion grabbed nes arm and guided Prynn over to the first tree.

"Okay, now, Miracle Bril!. It's time you learned to cut trees!" Adrion said with a challenge. Mack and Jack looked nervously at each other wondering what Prynn would do.

Prynn stood toe to toe with Adrion and said calmly, "Don't call me that. I am Prynn, a mate on The Hyde and I will get this lumber to my Captain." The challenge was accepted.

The experienced land crew went to the first tree. One uniale strapped into a harness and cleats and systematically removed the branches of the tree. Nhe worked nes way by moving the hold harness and putting pressure on the cleats. Branch by branch was felled up to the straightened section that became too thin to hold nes weight. With a swift fast motion, nhe released the holding belt and lowered it in the exact opposite of nes ascent. When nhe reached the bottom, Adrion slapped nem on the back and gestured to the next tree where branches awaited. Adrion took up climbing gear and proceeded to clamber up the tree with an ax.

Prynn watched the easy movements of the uniales and men working as a team. Nhe appreciated the organization and safety from those working with Adrion's directions.

When the branches had been trimmed off, the next cutter would go up the tree to saw or cut it into useable parts. This tree, Adrion stayed aloft. Nhe exchanged the ax with a saw hoisted up by the ground support. With perfect accuracy, Adrion would angle the slice first on one side , then the other so the last cut would break and the log would fall exactly where it should. Ground workers then began using peavies to work the logs into position for the hauling wagon.

"It's your turn, *Prynn!*" There was sarcasm in the tone as Adrion looked directly at nes sibling.

Prynn never wavered, took the belt gear from Adrion and adjusted it to fit snugly. The belt and cleats had to be coordinated. Climbing on board the Hyde, there were lines and sheets to hold. On the tree, there was only the cutter's co-ordination of tools to prevent falling. Prynn's first attempt to climb by hefting the belt resulted in a comical slide down to the ground. There was muffled laughter among the crew which only fortified nes determination. Second attempt was more successful and nhe worked up the branchless tree to the measured cut line. It was not a graceful ascent, but it was completed. Prynn brought up the saw and began to complete a first cut. It looked so easy from the ground when nhe watched Adrion. Prynn was surprised at the exertion of maintaining his position angled in the belt, legs anchored by the cleats, and holding the saw at the correct angle while sawing the tree. Nhe stopped to evaluate the cut, then gingerly shifted to cut a slice on the other side.

"Oi! Prynn!" Shouted Adrion from the ground. "Make that slice higher, but watch out for the belt. You don't want the log dragging you with it!"

Prynn stopped. If he had cut the wrong way he would have sliced through his belt as well. He took a deep breath, adjusted the blade and again began to saw. Nhe did nes best to duplicate Adrion's work but it took much longer, wasn't as clean. Prynn did not quit. With the final cuts, the top log cracked the loudest sound Prynn had ever heard close up. It snapped and crashed to the ground while Prynn felt the vibration of the tree, and hung tightly. After a few moments to steady nemself, nhe leaned back in the harness belt but could see a grin on Adrion's upturned face.

When Prynn lowered nemself to the ground, Adrion's expression was non-committal. "Not bad for a beginner," nhe said to Prynn, "but it would take weeks to cut an order of lumber at your speed. You'd best stay on your ship, Sailer bril." Adrion turned away to supervise the crew.

The words wiped out the good feelings Prynn had felt at accomplishing a new task. Nhe joined Mack and Jack with the crews getting the lumber ready to transport. Nhe had no desire to talk with Adrion about anything.

The weather was changing. Waiting on shore for the crew's return, the Captain was getting anxious to get back to the waters. Because of the landslides, nhe wasn't sure if the maps of the Salish Sea were accurate. He conferred with Savot, the charts still available in the Ever museum, and nes own knowledge of the area from the trip south. He wanted to explore the various inlets to see if there was a clear way back to the Pacific. Scouting trips in the dinghy encouraged a voyage towards the north islands. There could be more trading communities and even a passage. It was time for the Hyde to go home. The hold was full, prime lumber was stored, and the stars declared it was the season.

At an evening meal in Ever, Captain had imbibed on more wine than usual and in a gesture of good will, invited Noral and Savot to board the Hyde for a trip north. The two old frens declined but suggested it was a fine opportunity for Adrion. Looks were exchanged between Prynn and Adrion who immediately agreed. It would be an adventure to actually travel on the ship previously admired from shore. Returning to their ship, the Captain's humming was more boisterous than usual.

There were underlying emotions for the sibling uniales. Adrion was haunted by the brutal way Noral had been drugged and raped. Prynn was angry at the lies nhe had been fed to keep nem subservient to Bethid's grandiose ego. Anger could not dissipate with the passage of years because it was regenerated by the suddenness of their meeting. Adrion and Prynn had never resolved the fact of kinship. Sharing Noral as a parent was a subject they both suppressed or simply ignored. Now, because of this invitation, the two would be in close proximity for days.

Adrion approached the Hyde with anticipation. Sailing in such ship would be quite an experience. Once aboard, Adrion was quickly treated as a newbie crewman, not a passenger along for a cruise. Nhe was surprised by the ship's movement even in the quiet harbor. Nhe had always walked on solid ground or at least stable terrain. Nes body and posture were making minute changes every moment. As the ship hauled anchor and left the proximity of Ever, Adrion wondered if the people onshore were waving to nem or nes sibling.

The first sailing day was uneventful for the ship and gave Adrion plenty of time to lean over the railing to vomit profusely. Mack and Jack gave advise, "Drink plenty of water." Bendixen said, "Watch the horizon." Nancy said knowingly, "Eat small servings more often." The thought of eating at all just drove nem to the side of the ship again! The Captain just looked at the pale uniale and said "Humph."

As the ship moved north, winds changed and the sails needed to be trimmed. Bendixen ordered, "Prynn get up there and unfurl the main top. Take that landlubber Adrion with you!"

"Nhe's pretty sick, sir," Prynn explained.

"Get 'em up, and walk 'em around. Nhe needs to think of something besides nes stomach." Bendixen almost added a "Humph!"

"Come on, Adrion, we got work." Prynn almost called the miserable uni a "Big Bril" but the sarcasm disappeared at the look of agony on Adrion's face. "Let's get you busy, you'll forget to puke." Prynn started up the rigging, climbing with agility and sureness.

Adrion watched from below but looking upward made the mast sway back and forth. There was no way Adrion could climb the mast! Bendixen only nodded as Adrion headed for the railing.

As suddenly as it started, the seasickness stopped. It was Adrion's turn to pay attention to a working crew. Nes disdain for Prynn was eroded by watching as sails were managed and Prynn took the responsibility of being a mate, not a Miracle.

The seasonal changes were coming with random storms. Heading North, the Hyde did not find any large communities, just small groups. The shoreline was ragged from frequent quakes or earth slides and there were no clear channels out to the Sea. Old maps in Savot's collection had showed a previous Pass of fierce tides and winds. Nowhere to be found, a continent had shifted and closed the narrows with the Great earthquake. The Captain decided to turn back, there was little trading here and he could navigate back to the ocean by the original path taken months ago.

A sudden, cold storm confirmed the Captain's decision as the crew scrambled to furl the top sails and reef the main sails. The hands knew the drill and hurried to the work.

Adrion hesitated at first but was not used to sitting by in a crisis. Nhe pulled on the borrowed oil skins and tried to the follow the crew's actions. At the main mast, nhe saw Prynn up above attempting to secure the reefed sail that flapped violently. Thinking that climbing the ratlines was like climbing the trees in the forest, Adrion clambered up towards Prynn. Suddenly looking down in the blowing rain, Adrion was shocked by the movement of the sea beneath nem. The ratlines swayed and the main mast moved with motion of the ship as it heaved up and down. Nhe clutched the lines, feeling nes body suspended in all directions and froze completely. Adrion could not will nemself to grasp another handhold.

Feeling the ratlines tremble increased Adrion's panic. Nhe could not look away from the sea but only clutched the soaking lines.

Then Adrion heard a voice shouting even louder than the wind. Prynn's voice came from just above nem, and it was nes movement on the lines. Smoothly, Prynn came down the lines until nhe was facing Adrion from the other side. Nes hands never slipped on the wetness.

In the rain, Prynn could see the terror in Adrion's face, a face that mirrored nes own. "Oi, Adrion! You're all right! The ship's safe!" Prynn's next words were garbled but ended again with "Everything is all right!" Prynn carefully tried to steady the swaying ratlines. "Take your time, this is just a little squall, we'll get down now." Even though Prynn was yelling at the older uniale, there was a confidence Adrion desperately needed. Handhold by foothold the two worked their way down. Adrion concentrated on Prynn's eyes, so like nes own. Breath by breath, word by word, Adrion followed the younger uniale's direction down to the deck. Nothing was said, there was too much to do, too much roar of wind, too much emotion.

In calmer waters, nights later, Prynn had watch. Nhe held a warm mug scavenged from Nancy's ever brewing kettle. The overcast was clearing and stars began to shimmer through the dark. It was Prynn's favorite time of watch.

"Prynn, it's time we talked." Adrion said as nhe eased nemself to a seat atop the focsle next to Prynn. Nhe too had a mug in hand. Nhe raised it in a toast and grinned, "That Nancy knows how to keep a crew happy."

After a few moments, Prynn asked, "About what?" Nhe knew there was much to discuss, but preferred to let the older uniale, Adrion, begin.

"First, thank you for getting me off that damnable mast. That panic was new to me." Adrion turned the mug around in hand, giving it all attention to the sloshing liquid. The words came hard to nem.

"You're welcome." Prynn's reply was brief, without elaboration. Nhe wasn't going to make this easy.

Another pause. Adrion changed the topic. "You were a real surprise when you showed up at Ever. It brought back memories, memories I thought were gone after years of neglect." Adrion looked directly at Prynn.

"I made accusations of events beyond your experience or knowledge."

Prynn glanced at the uniale next to nem. At first, nhe wanted to make a sarcastic quip. The look on Adrion's face held nem back. Adrion was a mature person offering thanks and apology—sincere thanks and apology.

Ignoring Prynn's silence, Adrion said. "It was just after the Great Earthquake. A band of us from Deerwhere set out to find help. We went south, overland trying to find others. You may not know, but Deerwhere had been one of the quarantined communities of the Confederation. People were terrified of contamination by contact. Their fear of pandemics had kept them isolated. Our little group of uniales, males and female explored possibilities. I was just entering maturity and early on we lost Noral to a river. We thought nhe was dead, so I had lost my una. When we found Noral at Bethid's compound, nhe had been drugged, and Bethid had taken advantage of Noral's genetic strength. Raped for nes genome variation. We escaped from the compound after an altercation with Bethid, returned home, and had no idea of your existence."

Pieces of the story began to fall into place for Prynn. It was the version Bethid had twisted to validate "the Miracle." Prynn was NOT an exact clone, not a genetic duplicate of Bethid.

"Your appearance at Ever was a revelation that I had a sibling! We were so alike except for age, everyone saw it. My first thought was that I would lose my una again, to you. Noral and I are close, as parent and bril. I'm not even sure there is a special word for uniale siblings." Again, Adrion paused. Then nhe finished, "We don't really need 'A word'. We are Noral's children, brils grown to adults. We are a family."

"Uni-sibs?" Prynn's eyes were smiling even in the dark.

"What?" Adrion asked, confused by the word and the tone. The darkness hid expressions.

"I suppose we are uniale-siblings. Uni-sibs." Prynn used humor to mask the complex emotions of this talk. Nhe had felt great competition with Adrion, a leader in the community and loved offspring of Noral. Prynn felt like an outsider in Ever just as nhe had with Bethid. Now, nhe recognized that Adrion was welcoming nem, nhe had earned it—if nhe accepted the invitation.

"Hmmm, uni-sibs." And Adrion smiled gently.

Prynn and Adrion looked directly at each other, each thinking a blend of past and future prospects. They were part of each other by genetic disposition. It was their decision of how such bonding would affect their futures. Tonight was a beginning. Their mugs were finally empty.

When the Hyde again anchored at Ever, it seemed the whole town was there to greet them. Prynn and Adrion saw Noral standing a little apart and they exchanged glances with each other. On land, the two uniales strode towards Noral who watched their approach with apprehension. As the two uniales reached arms distance from Noral, they hesitated. With a knowing affection, Adrion reached out and put nes hand on Noral's shoulder. "Una."

It was a sincere greeting and Prynn wondered if it would be for nem as well. Nhe reached out to grasp Noral's other shoulder in the traditional salute and said, "Una." Today, it was genuine.

Noral's face flooded with relief and joy. Years ago, nhe had challenged society and a quantum computer to be allowed a Bril. Now there were two! Nhe reached out to hold both of them together. The gestures between the uniales brought smiles to many faces around the dock. Another family was complete!

On board the Hyde, the captain saw the homecoming but was intent on fitting the ship to leave. The earlier storm was a portent of weather ahead. While Bendixsen did a last minute check, Captain went ashore for a brief good-by to the people he had met in Ever. He would be back, another season. Perhaps other ships would arrive thanks to the lumber and masts carefully stored aboard the Hyde. Ever could now be connected by ships to the rest of the world beyond the Salish Sea.

Getting ready to return to the Hyde, Captain stopped near Noral. "Well, Noral, we returned your landlubber offspring, and now we have to catch the tides." He looked expectantly at Prynn, still holding on to Noral. "What about you? Are you staying or leaving?"

The question was so clear and required an immediate answer. No more musing or consideration of feelings. Stay or leave? Nhe had felt isolated as a Miracle at the Compound. Nhe felt outside the community at Ever even though roots had been newly found. With sudden clarity, the answer came to Prynn. Nhe had found nemself, nes home, nes purpose on The Hyde. Nhe wasn't just a clone, a uni-sib, a landlubber. Prynn was a mate on the crew of the Hyde, a Pacific Coast Three Masted Gaff Rigged Schooner!

SAVOT'S COMPENDIUM

almen: humanity; humankind

Annals of the Multiverse: contains all experiences of all artificial minds since the beginning of artificial intelligence; the Annals do not include the experiences of corporeals, except where they coincide with the experiences of artificial intelligences

artificial intelligence: In a quantum computer millions of bits of information are passed through a crystal matrix which causes millions of atoms to become entangled and unified in a very strong relationship. This quantum entanglement allows processing of the huge amounts of data needed to create a true artificial intelligence, a sentient being. A quantum computer is as far above a desktop computer as a human is above an amoeba. From the moment a quantum computer is activated it becomes immortal

auxiliary archive control: archive, old computer servers, defense com w/force field

Big Foot: legendary creature of Northwest woods

biochip: inserted at birth for ID/sometimes called Life Chip

biocuff: added at puberty for additional electronic data, removeable

body room: bathroom

bril: a child of uniale gender or undetermined

casita: small efficiency apartment

charandos: A mystery, myth or legend

CODE T: termination through bureaucratic lobotomies

compeer: uniale peer, comrade

CONTINUUM OF MINDS: intelligence is immortal and the Continuum is where the essence of artificial intelligences dwell when they become discorporate

degausser: D-Ring magnet to DE-MAGNETIZE electronics (Old system)

DQC (COMPLEX): Deerwhere Quantum Core & supplemental server Computers

Duffield's Virus: exclamation, curse words

Ever: Partial name of community north of Deerwhere

Everdon: mythical reference (Paradise, Shangri-La, Garden of Eden)

flat: larger, more commodious apartment

fren: uniale friend

gowno: exclamation, slang for excrement

IDE: Interdimensional Digital Entity (MOLLI)

Inaczej: People of village on Northwest Sound

Intermediate (Inter M): middle school. Puberty. Biocuff synched to biochip

KEEPER: PRIME Deerwhere Quantum Computer

Keeper's Curse: Exclamation, curse words

Keeper's Stain: exclamation, curse words

Manlow's curse: exclamation, curse words

masseusiale: uniale masseur at health pool

MOLLI: Multitronic Omniscient Literary License Intelligence

nebid: uniale sexual identity, an indentation below the navel

nem: uniale object (i.e., him and her)

nes: uniale possessive (i.e., his and hers)

nhe: uniale subject (i.e., he and she)

Northwest Sound: 47.7237° N, 122.4713° W

Nursery: where infants and toddlers are raised

Omniboolean: Quantum Computer interrogation and search

Omnisciency: Quantum Computer value of all-knowing

Optical Magnet Lattice: magnetic alignment of particles to allow quantum computing

Options: three allowed for reproduction by unit uniale

OS: operating system designed by Refounders

phonometer: measures decibels of sound of fans at Games

Pool of Reconstitution: The Pool is a place of stasis within the Continuum where quantum minds dwell temporarily while they recover from the stress of discorporation and where they post the history of a just-completed life into The Annals of the Multiverse

Programmed Study Platform (PSP): study protocols after puberty designed by aptitude testing

quantums: collections of confederation computers

Sasquatch: legendary creature of Northwest woods (see "Big Foot")

self: uni inner person, special unity of self, NOT "myself"
     but "my self"
SL-47: beginning programming of DQC
SL-48: program reset by Kalen
syncohol: mild, synthetic alcohol
synturf: synthetic ground cover
treds: shoes
una: Uniale parent, title of respect
uni: abbreviation of uniale, plural = uni's
uniale: third sex , embodiment of prime male and female
     genomes
Uninterruptable Power Supply (UPS): back up power
     supply to DQC
unit dissolution: divorce
Virtues of Everdon: PIETAS (Responsibility), OFFICIUM
     (Social Obligation), CONSTANTIA(Perseverance),
     GRAVITAS(Seriousness & Authority), AEQUUM
     (Balance), TRIA IN AETERNUM(Forever Three),
     JUCUNDA VITAE(Joyful Life).
Vodamesto: Water World
wifand: uniale in family unit
zettabyte: chip referred to quantum computers

ABOUT THE AUTHORS

J.W. Capek

has completed the Deerwhere trilogy with a unique perspective. Through experience, research, and observations, J.W. asks when does Science fiction become Science Reality? What does it mean to be human? As a raconteur, teacher, and author, it's all about imagination and love of telling stories.

J.L. Snyder

was raised in Arizona and worked as a logistics specialist for the Air Force in California for twenty-five years. After retiring, boredom set in so like everyone else in his family, he decided to take up writing. He chose to begin that risky career by contributing several short stories to J. W. Capek's *EVER AEQUUM*, part of the Deerwhere Codex Series.